OLD-FAS

JE

MW01257318

Thanks!
Jenna!

Jenna St. James Books

Ryli Sinclair Mystery Series Order

Picture Perfect Murder
Girls' Night Out Murder
Old-Fashioned Murder
Bed, Breakfast, and Murder
Veiled in Murder
Bachelorettes and Bodies
Rings, Veils, and Murder
Last Stop Murder

Sullivan Sisters Mystery Series Order

Murder on the Vine
Burning Hot Murder
Prepear to Die

DEDICATION

To my mom, Sue Buhman. Your unwavering love and encouragement is such a blessing.

To my sister, Juliana Buhman. Thank you for putting up with my crazy cover critiques.

To Whitney and Megan. I hope I did your friendship justice. Drinks at my house!

And to my cousin, Thomas Shifflett. Thanks for being such a good sport.

CHAPTER 1

Aunt Shirley crossed her arms over her sagging chest and scowled at me. "I'm telling you it's a story."

"And I'm telling *you* that a couple of residents at Oak Grove Manor talking about a missing box in the pantry is *not* a story." I slammed my desk drawer shut and wondered again for the thousandth time why my boss, Hank Perkins, had hired my crazy great-Aunt Shirley last month to work for the town paper.

I know why *I* worked for *The Granville Gazette,* the one and only newspaper in Granville, Missouri. Six years ago I graduated college with a major in journalism and a minor in photography. Soon after, I needed to pay back student loans and this was the only job I could find. I stay at the *Gazette* because I need to make enough money to pay my brother, Matt, rent on the one-bedroom, eight hundred square foot cottage he lets me rent from him.

Aunt Shirley's only claim to fame was the fact she used to be a private investigator out in California decades ago. That's it. She has no background in anything other than stakeouts and telling whoppers about how she used to date and sleep with all the hottest Hollywood male stars back in the day.

"And I'm telling you you're wrong," Aunt Shirley insisted. "Not only have recently shipped boxes gone missing from the pantry, but Old Man Jenkins told me his bottle of Viagra was stolen out of his room last week. It seems we have some sticky fingers at the Manor."

I shuddered at the thought that Old Man Jenkins needed Viagra pills and that my Aunt Shirley had a first-hand account of that information.

Aunt Shirley rolled her eyes at my reaction. "You're such a child, Ryli."

"I'm twenty-eight. That doesn't qualify me as a child."

"A prude then," Aunt Shirley insisted.

"I have work to do. Could you please be quiet and let me think."

Aunt Shirley went on as though I hadn't spoken. "I think we have a burglary ring, and I think the ring leader is Sheri Daniels, the Coordinator at the Manor."

I sighed, knowing if I didn't humor her a little bit, she'd never let it go. "Why do you think this Sheri Daniels is the ring leader?"

"She's constantly threatening to kick me out. I think she's threatened by the fact I'm a private investigator. She knows it's only a matter of time before I sniff out her burglary ring and she and her minions go down."

"First off, you're a *former* private investigator," I said. "And secondly, who are these minions?"

Aunt Shirley scowled at me. "I'm not sure who else she has working for her, but I bet if we put our heads together, we could solve this case. Then think of the story we could write for the *Gazette*."

"There is no case," I said, "and there is no story."

"Those old people would think we were the bee's knees."

I politely refrained from reminding my Aunt Shirley that she was one of those "old" people that lived at Oak Grove Manor. The

Manor isn't a traditional nursing home. It's an assisted living facility for the elderly. Aunt Shirley was put there over a year ago by both my mom and Police Chief Garrett Kimble—who also happens to be my boyfriend. It seems nearly burning your house down when raking leaves, going into town without pants on, and attacking and beating up said chief of police—although he'd deny it now—will get you a life sentence in an assisted living facility. Mom sold Aunt Shirley's house and the proceeds from the sale keep her living at the Manor.

"If you don't want to run with the stolen goods," Aunt Shirley sulked, "what else we got?"

"*We* don't have anything. *I'm* trying to brainstorm ideas if you'd stop yammering away in my ear."

Ever since I helped capture two different killers in three months, Hank has pretty much let me take on a bigger role at the newspaper. Last week he told me I could have the front-page spot for Valentine's Day if I could pitch him a worthwhile story, and I didn't want to let him down.

My boss, Hank Perkins, is a retired Marine who still walks the walk and talks the talk. Once a Marine, always a Marine. Oorah! He was fifty-two years old, mean as the day was long, and didn't give a darn about anything except his wife and his newspaper.

Mindy, his wife, was his opposite in every way. She was as gentle and kind as he was mean. She had platinum blonde hair that was teased for miles, and she wore skin-tight Capri pants and neon colored off-the-shoulder shirts or sweaters. And no matter what the Missouri weather was outside, she always wore designer high-heeled shoes.

I heard the click-click of Mindy's shoes before I saw her. "Now, now girls," Mindy said kindly as she set a cup of herbal tea down in front of me. "Let's not fight today."

I wanted to tell Mindy that Aunt Shirley had started it, but I took the high road and refrained.

"Ryli started it," Aunt Shirley said.

I threw down my pen, plunked my head on the desk, and cursed Hank for the thousandth and one time that day for hiring Aunt Shirley. I knew he hired her because it doubled his chances of getting a good story—Aunt Shirley and I are notorious at being magnets for disaster.

Mindy chuckled. "Let me see what you've come up with and see if I can help." Mindy picked up my scratch paper and began reading.

"Personally," Aunt Shirley piped up, "I think there's a story with the stolen goods at the Manor, but Lois Lane here doesn't want to hear it."

I closed my eyes and waited for Mindy to say something…anything.

"I kind of like this idea of love in different stages of life," Mindy said. "Of course I'm partial to love stories because I married my one true love."

Aunt Shirley made a gagging sound.

"Maybe you could do a 'love through the ages' sort of story," Mindy suggested. "Think about it. You have young love with Matt and Paige, seeing as how they've only been married a little over a month. You could interview them. Then maybe find another couple that's been married for fifty years. Maybe even do an interview with a widow or widower and talk about the struggle of going on *without* your true love."

"That's a great idea," I said.

Hank's office door flew open. He leaned against the doorjamb and yanked the unlit cigar out of his mouth. "Hey Shirley Temples…instead of sitting here on your butts all day, how about you get out there and do what I pay you to do. I just received word there's a fire on Fifth Street."

I jumped up from my desk and scowled at him. I hated it when he called Aunt Shirley and me Shirley Temples. It was insulting—to us, and the sickening-sweet-no-punch-to-it drink he liked to think we were.

Aunt Shirley hooted and grabbed her camo parka. "You heard the man, Lois Lane. Let's roll."

I sighed and grabbed my coat and camera. They should call me Rodney Dangerfield because I get no respect.

I opened the door of my 1965 turquoise Ford Falcon and turned over the engine. It's really Aunt Shirley's car, but since she's no longer allowed to legally drive, it's mine now. I'd coveted this car since I was a little girl. Under the hood was a stock 302 with an Edelbrock fuel injection. The interior was just as sweet. The barely-there dashboard was done in the same turquoise color, and the bucket seats in the front and bench seat in the back were pristine white with turquoise stitching.

I pulled out of the parking lot of the newspaper office and slowly headed toward Fifth Street. There was still snow on the ground from the snowstorm we'd had last week.

Granville has a population of just over ten thousand, and is made up of two main streets, Elm and Pike. They meet in the heart of downtown at a four-way stop. On the downtown square we have the courthouse, a couple banks, a sub shop, two café-type restaurants, and a handful of antiques stores. It's also where Legends Salon and Nails is located, but it's recently been under new ownership since the previous owner, Iris Newman, went and got herself murdered a couple months back.

On the outskirts of town going west, we have a Burger Barn, the elementary, middle, and high schools, along with a small hospital. On the east side of town we have a small family-run grocery store, the police station, and the newspaper building where I work.

Fifth Street is lined with rows of houses that pretty much all look alike. Most were small, run-down, two-story dwellings that still had asbestos siding on them. There were a handful of neighbors huddled together on the sidewalk speculating on what was going on. I didn't see any flames, so I figured it wasn't much of a house fire.

I pulled up about four car lengths behind the fire truck, and Aunt Shirley and I made our way toward the firemen and Garrett. I took a couple pictures with my camera, while Aunt Shirley took a selfie of herself with the fire trucks in the background. Aunt Shirley was in charge of all the social media accounts the *Granville Gazette* had. She'd do a teaser online and I'd write a story for the paper.

"Hi. Ryli Sinclair, reporter for the *Granville Gazette*," I said flirtatiously to Garrett. "Can I get a quote about what's happened here?"

Garrett Kimble is ten years older than me, with jet-black hair styled short from his military days, and the bluest eyes I've ever seen. He's been the Chief now for a year and a half. After leaving active duty, he worked for the Kansas City Police Department until my brother, Matt, talked him into applying for the job opening in Granville. He and Matt met at a veterans convention.

Aunt Shirley snorted behind me. "Stop flirting and let him get to the good stuff. What's the scoop here, Ace?"

Garrett's jaw clenched but let the name-calling slide. "Nothing to tell. Seems the owner just forgot about some bacon in the oven. The grease had fallen onto the oven burners and black smoke was rolling. When the homeowner opened the oven door to get the bacon out, the smoke filled the kitchen, and she opened a window. Unfortunately her neighbor happened to be outside and thought there was a fire."

"Well, now that's disappointing," Aunt Shirley pouted. "Not that I want anyone hurt, but I guess the only story here is that someone can't cook."

"Hey," I objected, "accidents happen. I wouldn't say it means she doesn't know how to cook."

Aunt Shirley snorted. "Says the numbskull who doesn't know the difference between cream of tartar and tartar sauce."

Again, I get no respect. You make one little mistake and the whole world remembers.

Garrett reached over and gave me a one-arm hug. "I wouldn't poke too much fun. I seem to remember someone setting her own place on fire after raking leaves naked."

Okay, maybe I get a little respect.

CHAPTER 2

"Not that I wanted it to be a house fire," I sighed, kicking snow off my shoes before getting in the Falcon, "but we really need a story." I turned over the Falcon and headed toward Oak Grove Manor on Cherry Street to drop Aunt Shirley off. It was four o'clock, and I was ready to put my feet up and have a glass of wine.

"Phew, you stink like charcoaled bacon," Aunt Shirley complained.

I lifted up my sweater and sniffed. She was right. I did stink. And if there was one smell I knew, it was burned food smell. I definitely needed a shower and a large glass of wine. I was due at Mom's for dinner around seven.

"I'll just drop you off and see you tomorrow." I pulled into the circle drive and idled the car. Oak Grove Manor was an old, rundown, three-story brick building with patches of ivy clinging to the exterior. While the groundskeepers obviously tried keeping the outside up, there was no denying the dilapidated feel of the Manor. The only saving grace of the place was the fact a few of the apartments had tiny balconies that looked like one person could squeeze onto them.

"No can do, Missy. I need you to come upstairs and move something for me," Aunt Shirley said. "Park over in the visitor area and come on up."

I didn't want to go up to Aunt Shirley's apartment because I was afraid she'd keep me there. I understand she's lonely sometimes, but she lives in a huge building full of people she could make friends with if she just tried.

"What on Earth could you have to move?" I asked. "You don't have anything in that sparse apartment."

When she first moved in, Aunt Shirley refused to decorate the place, claiming she wasn't going to be there for more than a few months, so why waste the energy. She was now going on a year and half at the Manor. A year and a half with no major furniture or decorations, and really no friends to speak of.

I dropped Aunt Shirley off at the front doors, then zipped into an empty parking space in the visitor's section. I bundled my coat around me and jogged to the glass double doors. The inside of the Manor opens to a massive lobby complete with an information desk, three couches, a big screen wall-mounted TV, a reading nook by a fireplace, and a checkers table in front of a large bay window overlooking a small pond in the back of the Manor. Off to the side of the pond was a courtyard and greenhouse.

A row of windows separated the lobby from the cafeteria. Already I could see a few folks eating at the tables. Must be the early, early-bird special.

I waved to a couple residents I recognized and even a few of the orderlies. I'd been around long enough to be familiar with the ins and outs of the Manor.

I saw Old Man Jenkins playing checkers with another elderly man in front of the window and made my way over to say hello. Old Man Jenkins was ninety if he was a day, short, bald, and was built like a strong wind would knock him over. Why in the world he was attracted to Aunt Shirley I had no idea. She towered over him by a foot, outweighed him by a good thirty pounds, and had a mouth on her a sailor would envy.

Mr. Jenkins smiled when I stopped at his table. "Ryli Sinclair, I swear you look more and more like your aunt every day."

I shuddered at the thought but forced a smile at him and his checkers partner.

"This here is Andy O'Brien," Old Man Jenkins said. "He's a terrible checkers player but one of my oldest friends."

Mr. O'Brien stuck his wrinkled hand out to me. I clasped it, careful not to squeeze too hard. They both looked like they could break in half at any time.

"Anything new going on today?" I asked.

"Well, did you hear about my bottle of Viagra getting stolen?" Old Man Jenkins asked.

Oh boy!

I was saved from a reply when he looked over his shoulders before leaning in. "Whole lot more than Viagra getting stolen around here lately, too."

My ears perked up. Could Aunt Shirley really be on to something? "Like what? I know Aunt Shirley said some boxes in the pantry were stolen, and your...pills. What else?"

Mr. O'Brien leaned forward. "Quite a few things actually, my dear."

Old Man Jenkins nodded in agreement. "According to my sources, jewelry, money out of wallets, medications. Things like that."

"Your sources?" I asked with a smile.

Old Man Jenkins gave me a wicked grin. "Your aunt asked me to keep my ear to the ground. Said she'd make it worth my while."

I suppressed a groan. I knew that usually meant Aunt Shirley would show him a certain body part of hers. "What's significant about the boxes from the pantry?"

Mr. Jenkins and Mr. O'Brien looked at each other and shrugged.

"No idea," Old Man Jenkins said. "And most of the thefts have occurred in our private rooms. This is the first theft I've heard about venturing out into the Manor itself."

"Any idea who's behind the thefts?" I asked.

"Nope. That's where your aunt and you come in," Mr. Jenkins said. "We let you girls handle the investigative work."

I thanked the men and made my way out of the lobby and toward Aunt Shirley's wing. She lived on the third floor of the Tropical Paradise wing.

I passed a partially closed door with a plaque touting the name Sheri Daniels on it. I'd never really met Oak Grove Manor's Coordinator, but I had to admit I was curious now that she might be the leader in a burglary ring.

I heard crying and yelling going on inside the room.

"I don't care to listen to your sniveling anymore, Kaylee. You'd better find those boxes and find them now!"

The stolen boxes from the pantry?

I paused, looked around to make sure no one was watching, and placed my ear close to the partially closed door. I could hear a female crying.

"I'm so sorry, Sheri. I honestly don't know what's happened to them. I've looked everywhere!"

"You were the last person to handle the boxes, so they are your responsibility. If you don't find them soon, you're fired!"

More sobbing. I'm assuming from this Kaylee person who lost the shipment. "Please, Sheri, I really need this job. It's just me trying to support my baby."

"Not my problem. I had you place the order, it was delivered, you put it in the pantry, and now it's gone missing. You were the last one to see the boxes."

"And I'm telling you," Kaylee insisted between sniffles, "I stacked the boxes in the walk-in pantry just like you told me to."

14

"And what? They just got up and walked away?"

Man, this Sheri Daniels really is a colossal witch! I thought Aunt Shirley was exaggerating.

"You better find the shipment, Kaylee, or your days here at Oak Grove Manor are numbered." Sheri said. "Now get out."

In a panic, I flattened myself against the wall, my back next to the open door. If Kaylee looked to her right she'd see me, but I didn't know what else to do.

Luckily I didn't have to worry. Poor Kaylee came rushing out the door, sobbing into her hand. She never looked my way.

"And what about my stuff?" a male voice said angrily. "Did you get it reordered?"

"Yes, Mr. Manning, I got it reordered. It should be here in a couple days."

"It better be," Manning growled.

"I said it's coming," Sheri said icily. "Now please get out so I can go back to work."

I figured that was my hint to hightail it out of there unless I wanted to get caught. And I didn't want to run into Aunt Shirley's surly neighbor, Mr. Manning, either. He was a whole lot of trouble.

I walked through the swinging doors of the extra-wide corridor that was decorated with fake plants, palm trees, and walls covered in faded pictures of tropical islands and beaches. I heard the swish of the swinging doors as they closed behind me.

"Mr. Manning!" I recognized Kaylee's voice.

I looked around to find a place to hide, but there was nothing around me in the sparse hallway. I flattened myself against the wall adjacent to the swinging doors to try and hide. I prayed the doors would not come back and hit me in the face.

"What do you want?" Mr. Manning growled.

"You knew I put those boxes in the pantry," Kaylee said. "Did you take them?"

Manning laughed. "A lot of people knew you put the boxes in the pantry. It's not like it's a big secret. But word of advice, you might want to find them before I do. Because I'll make sure you're fired. That means you'll be without a job, and your little brat will starve."

I held my breath as Manning pushed open the doors and stalked down the hallway toward the elevators.

"Not if I kill you first," Kaylee whispered.

I waited until everything had settled down before pushing myself off the wall. Who knew the Manor was such a breeding ground for drama?

I took the elevator to the third floor and walked to Aunt Shirley's apartment. The third floor had six apartments on it—three on each side. Aunt Shirley's apartment was the first apartment on the left-hand side, apartment number 366. I always wondered how hard it would be to turn the three into a six.

The door across the hall and over one from Aunt Shirley's place was open, and I could hear women's laughter inside. I was about to peek in when Aunt Shirley's door flew open.

"It's about time," Aunt Shirley wheezed through the vapor of her electronic cigarette. "What took you so long?"

She yanked on my coat and pulled me into her apartment. The living quarters consisted of a tiny kitchen, breakfast nook barely big enough for two people, and a living room sporting a sofa, recliner, coffee table, and TV.

That's it.

There are no pictures or other decorations anywhere. The bedroom and bathroom were located down a narrow hallway to the left of the open archway. As luck would have it, Aunt Shirley was one of the lucky ones that had one of those barely-there balconies.

"I see you're still smoking that ridiculous thing," I said. I didn't want to answer her question about what took me so long because I didn't want to admit I ran into Old Man Jenkins and that she may be on to something with the thefts. Aunt Shirley puffed on the e-cig and started to cough.

Aunt Shirley never smoked a day in her life. The fact there wasn't nicotine in the contraption she was using made it even more ridiculous for her to puff away on it.

"You look ridiculous," I said.

"If I wanted someone to nag me, I'd be married. Get in here and help me."

I sighed and took off my jacket, hanging it up over the back of one of the chairs. "Can I have a drink?"

Aunt Shirley walked into the kitchen, flipped on the light, took down two shot glasses from the cabinet, opened the freezer, and took out a bottle of tequila. My Aunt Shirley loved her tequila.

"I'm not drinking tequila," I said. "Don't you have anything else?"

"Nope. It's tequila or you drink water."

I sighed. "Fine, what do you have to mix it with?"

Aunt Shirley snorted. "Mix it with? I plan on mixing it with my saliva." She poured a shot, picked up her glass, and downed it in one gulp.

"I'll pass then." My aunt, the quintessential party girl. "So what did you need help moving? I need to get home."

"Let's watch that show with the hunky investigator guy. Mmm...mmm...I'd be his baby girl any night!" Aunt Shirley cackled wickedly as she grabbed the bottle and pushed past me to the living room.

I had to give her that one. If I didn't have Garrett, I'd definitely like to be Shemar Moore's baby girl.

I covered my ears when Aunt Shirley turned on the TV. The volume level was deafening, and I needed my eardrums to hear all the naughty things Garrett would be whispering in them later. "Turn it down. Jeez!"

Bang! Bang! Bang!

"I'll get it," I hollered. "You just work on turning it down."

I looked out the peephole and saw the protruding forehead and deep scowl of Aunt Shirley's horrendous neighbor, Ray Manning.

"Open up you battleax!" Manning lifted his cane and beat it against the door again.

Bang! Bang! Bang!

I stumbled back from the door, startled by the rage coming from Mr. Manning.

"I know you're in there!" Manning yelled. "I can hear your TV!"

"Turn it off!" I screamed at Aunt Shirley. "I can't take much more of this insanity."

"Fine," Aunt Shirley grumbled, clicking off the TV. "But take it from me, when Manning gets like this, the best thing to do is turn the volume up more. It drowns the old coot out."

Bang! Bang! Bang!

"Hold on!" I yelled.

I yanked open the door and scowled at Ray Manning. I'd only had a few run-ins with him since Aunt Shirley started staying at the Manor, but one thing was certain, he was a mean and unhappy man. From the conversation and death threat I overheard downstairs, I'd say I wasn't the only person that felt that way, either.

Old-Fashioned Murder

He was around eighty years old, five foot ten, bald except for a patch of white hair running around the back of his skull, and probably weighed one hundred eighty pounds. For an old guy, he was pretty intimidating.

I wanted to take the cane he was using to beat on the door and beat him over the head with it.

Obviously I needed a drink worse than I thought if I was willing to take a life over banging a cane on a door. Or I needed space from Aunt Shirley. Her I-hate-everyone attitude was rubbing off on me.

"What do you want, Mr. Manning?" I asked as politely as I could.

Ray Manning thumped his cane repeatedly on the floor. Obviously the guy needed to slow down on his consumption of caffeine and take an anger management class or two.

"I want you to turn that TV down! I've called down to the front desk and told them I've had enough. Either that horrible woman goes or I go!"

"Well, hate to see ya leave, old man," Aunt Shirley hollered from the living room. "But this floor will be a lot better off without your crotchety old carcass here."

Ray Manning's face turned red. He leaned down on his cane until he was eye level with me. "You might want to tell your aunt to watch her mouth."

"And you might want to back that nasty breath up before I keel over." I slapped my hand over my mouth, horrified that I'd spoken to someone like that. My momma raised me better!

Aunt Shirley cackled behind me. "You tell him, girl."

Ray Manning straightened and turned his hateful glare on Aunt Shirley. "I'd watch it if I were you. You won't look so good if you go missing some teeth."

I sucked in my breath. Had he seriously just threatened Aunt Shirley? A part of me was truly terrified by the old man...but another part of me was ready for Aunt Shirley to deliver a beatdown on the guy.

Aunt Shirley shoved me aside and got within an inch of Ray Manning. "I can promise you if you try to raise a hand to me, I'll break it and every other bone in your body!"

CHAPTER 3

The dinging of the elevator saved Aunt Shirley from a trip to the pokey. I had no doubt she was about to go all spider monkey on Ray Manning, which would result in an arrest. Something that would give Garrett great pleasure, but would just end up being a big hassle for me.

I groaned when Thomas Shifley—aka Shifty—got off the elevator and waddled over to where we were. I'd gone to high school with Shifley. He earned his unfortunate nickname in high school, and the name had stuck ever since. Numerous people at the Manor called him Shifty...sometimes to his face...sometimes behind his back.

"What's going on here?" Shifty demanded, narrowing his dark, beady eyes at Aunt Shirley.

"Nothing's going on here, Shifty," Aunt Shirley snarled. "Mind your own business."

Thomas Shifley ran his hands through his shaggy, oily hair and drew himself up to full height—which now made him about five foot four. "Listen here, Lady. I told you one more complaint and you're out."

I'm not gonna lie. Those words sent me into panic mode. No way was I going to have Aunt Shirley living with me. No way!

"Mr. Shifley," I cooed as best I could without gagging, "there's no problem here. Aunt Shirley just forgot to put in her hearing aids. We turned the TV down immediately."

"The day I need hearing aids is the day you need to take me out back and shoot me!"

"That could be arranged," Ray Manning said.

"That's it, Manning," Aunt Shirley snapped. "I could kill you right now in five different ways. So you might want to watch yourself."

Thomas Shifley's eyes bugged out of his head. "I don't think death threats are necessary here."

"That's part of your problem, Shifty," Aunt Shirley said. "You don't think."

I groaned. I could tell by the three shades of purple Shifley's face was turning that this was not going to end well for Aunt Shirley and me.

Thomas Shifley pointed his finger in Aunt Shirley's face. "That's it. I'm going to make sure you're out of here soon."

"Sticks and stones, Shifty...sticks and stones." Aunt Shirley slammed the door in their faces and cackled.

Breathe in, breathe out. Breathe in, breathe out.

"I'm not sure that was the smartest thing to do," I whispered.

"Pshaw! Shifty ain't gonna do nothing. You worry too much."

"And you worry too little," I countered.

I nearly fainted when a knock sounded at the door a few minutes later. I was positive it was Thomas Shifley coming back with reinforcements to kick Aunt Shirley out. I leaned in and peered through the peephole, breathing a sigh of relief when I saw it was Aunt Shirley's neighbors from across the hall. I'd only seen them in passing. I'd never stopped to talk with them.

I turned to whisper to Aunt Shirley. "It's your neighbors from across the hall. I'm going to let them in."

"Why? I don't talk to them. They're always trying to push their crap off on me."

I rolled my eyes and opened the door. "Hello, ladies. Won't you come in?"

"Thank you, dear. That's very kind of you," the shorter of the two said as she rolled in a cart, three tiers high. "My name is Lavinia Howk, but my friends call me Lovey. And this is Dorothea Cook, but we call her Dotty."

I guessed them to be around Aunt Shirley's age. Probably early seventies, but I couldn't be sure. Other than being similar in age, Lovey and Dotty were complete opposites.

Where Lovey was short, barely coming to my chest, I put Dotty at nearly six feet tall. Lovey was curvier and softer than Dotty's tall, straight form. Lovey had round facial features that made her look jovial and happy. Dotty's face was hawk-like and angular.

I stuck out my hand. "I'm Ryli, Aunt Shirley's great-niece."

"Humph," Aunt Shirley said. "Only sometimes are you a great niece." She laughed at her own joke.

I rolled my eyes.

"We couldn't help but overhear the arguing just now," Lovey said sympathetically. "I hope everything is okay. That Thomas Shifley can be difficult sometimes."

"And don't even get us started on Ray Manning," Dotty added in a gravelly voice. "That man is a nuisance. Always has been. Lovey and I have known him for over forty years. We've lived in Granville our whole lives, you know."

Aunt Shirley poured herself another shot of tequila. "I ain't worried about either one of them lowlifes." She tipped her head back and downed the drink.

"Ray Manning is not someone you want to tangle with," Lovey advised. "We're positive he's the one that's leaving horrible, threatening letters on Virginia's door. We just can't catch him in the act."

"That's horrible," I said. I had no idea who Virginia was, but I didn't want to dwell on what had just happened for fear it would lead to Aunt Shirley's removal. "What have you got here?"

Lovey clapped her small hands in glee. "Dotty and I are the hospitality wagon for the Manor. We go around and try to provide residents with things they might not be able to get their hands on otherwise. Sheri Daniels orders things off the Internet for residents, but if you are looking for something a little different, we're usually your girls." Lovey bent down and pulled a multi-colored afghan out of one of the tiers. "Here's one of our afghans we recently made."

I reached out and gingerly touched the blanket. "It's stunning."

"Lovey and I have been crocheting since we were kids," Dotty said as she stooped down and slid out another tier for me to investigate. "Here we have some chocolates that we've made. Plus we have other goodies like dandelion wine, magazines, and an assortment of other snacks. The food here isn't the best."

I laughed. "That's quite an eclectic assortment. I've never heard of dandelion wine."

"It's what a lot of us oldies grew up on," Lovey supplied.

"Remember when we'd go out in Virginia's pasture and pick those dandelions?" Dotty reminisced. "Virginia Webber is our other bestie, and she lives next door to us. She's the one that's getting the horrible letters from Ray Manning. She also has the unfortunate pleasure of living directly across the hall from him."

"Ha!" Aunt Shirley said. "Try living next door to him."

I smiled at Lovey and Dotty. "You guys are best friends and you all live together? That's so awesome!"

Lovey nodded. "Virginia has her own apartment, but Dotty and I share an apartment. We've all been friends about sixty years now."

"Wow, that's super cool. I hope my best friend, Paige, and I are friends sixty years from now!"

Lovey and Dotty smiled at each other.

"Is there anything we can get for you, Shirley?" Lovey asked as she put the afghan away.

"Nope. I got my stash of tequila, and that's all I need."

Dotty chuckled and shook her head. "We've been trying for a year now to expand your aunt's palate. There's more to drink than tequila."

"What do you drink?" I asked.

Dotty pulled a flask out of the pocket of her old-lady sweater.

Does every old person carry a flask? Is it some kind of old-person initiation?

"Today I'm drinking a Manhattan," Dotty said. "But Lovey, Virginia, and I also like to drink a Tom Collins, an Old Fashioned, and a Dirty Martini."

"I've heard of a couple of those drinks," I laughed.

"How about you, Ryli?" Lovey asked kindly. "Is there anything we can get for you?"

I sighed and thought about my looming deadline for the paper. "Seeing as how I work for the *Granville Gazette,* how about a front-page story idea for next week's Valentine's Day feature?"

Lovey lifted an eyebrow then looked up at Dotty.

"Well," Lovey said hesitantly, "it might not be what you're looking for, but Virginia has quite a story about love. Loves, actually."

I was immediately intrigued. "Really? What kind of story?"

Dotty took another drink of her Manhattan before answering. "Well, she's been married three times, and tragically all three husbands have died."

"Wow," I said, somewhat horrified at the thought. "I'm not sure how that's a love story."

Lovey reached over and patted my shoulder. "Oh, honey, it takes a lot for a woman to bounce back after one husband dies, but the fact she did it two more times is amazing. She opened herself up each time, and each time tragedy struck."

I frowned. "Okay. I think I see where you're going with this." The more I thought about it, the more I liked the idea. "Do you think she'd talk with me?"

Lovey shrugged. "I don't see why not. I'll tell you what, when we see her later on, we'll mention you'd like to talk with her."

I grabbed a pen and paper off the counter in Aunt Shirley's kitchen. "Here's my number. Have her call me if she's interested in talking."

Dotty took the paper from me, folded it, and slipped it in her pocket with the flask. "We better head out. We have a couple chocolate deliveries to make. Valentine's Day is a popular time for us."

I laughed and opened the door to let them out. "Thank you so much for everything. I hope to hear from Virginia soon."

I closed the door behind them and turned to Aunt Shirley. "I think this might be a good idea."

Aunt Shirley shrugged and took another shot of tequila.

"You need to slow down. And maybe it wouldn't hurt to expand your palate like Lovey and Dotty suggested."

"Pshaw. Why would I want to listen to those two goody-goody gasbags?"

"I thought they were great. You should get to know them better."

I heard knocking next door. It sounded like they were trying to peddle their wares to Mr. Manning. Good thing they'd had a stiff drink beforehand.

"I don't really like them," Aunt Shirley said.

"You don't really like anyone."

"True. So, your mom having dinner tonight?"

I knew this was a needle for an invitation. "Yes."

"Well, why didn't you say so? Let me change my clothes real quick and we'll head on over."

"Why did you even have me bring you here if your plan was all along to go to Mom's for dinner?"

Aunt Shirley grinned. "Because I didn't want to go over smelling like charcoaled bacon from the house fire."

CHAPTER 4

"I think it sounds like a great story," Paige said as she set the platter of roast on Mom's dinner table. "Imagine having been married three times and all three times your spouse dies. That's such a tragedy." She paused in thought. "Then again, maybe this isn't such a good idea for a Valentine's Day story."

I placed a bowl of cooked carrots next to the roast. I was trying to be as helpful as possible. When I came in with Aunt Shirley on my heels, Mom looked like she'd swallowed a lemon.

I stepped back and started making room on the table for more food. "I think I can spin it into a true love story spanning the years. I've had time to think about it, and I'm going to make the article all about her. This woman has put herself out there and loved three men. That takes a lot of courage."

Aunt Shirley plopped down on an empty chair at the table. "And do we know *how* these men died?" She nonchalantly reached down into her bra and pulled out a heart-shaped flask that read, "Tequila *is* my Boyfriend!" and took a nip from it.

I laughed. "Where did you get that hideous thing?"

Aunt Shirley grinned and thrust the flask toward me. "You like? One of my many Valentine's Day gifts to myself."

Paige rolled her eyes at me. "I thought having a purse that doubled as a flask was bad, but that thing is just plain tacky."

Aunt Shirley laughed and took another nip from the heart-shaped flask before capping it and putting it back inside her bra. "So, like I was saying, do we even know *how* these men died? Because this seems awfully suspicious to me. I could be living across the hall from a man killer. An actual Black Widow!"

"Slow your roll there, Aunt Shirley" I said. "First off, I'm sure if she offed three husbands, someone around here would have said something. You heard Lovey say the three of them have pretty much lived their whole lives here in Granville."

Paige giggled. "I still can't imagine being called Lovey. That's so odd. Cute...but odd."

"It kinda fits her though," I said. "She and Dotty are so nice. Making gifts and bringing items around for the people who can't get out as much."

Aunt Shirley belched loudly...a sure sign she was on the verge of getting tipsy. "More like goody-goody gasbags!"

"Stop," I said and gave her my best evil eye. "I like these ladies. You be nice or I won't invite you to the interview if Virginia Webber calls and says it's a go."

Aunt Shirley rolled her eyes. "Whatever. Where is everyone? I'm starving."

Mom glided effortlessly into the dining room balancing two heaping bowls of mashed potatoes. Her boyfriend, Dr. Powell, a local veterinarian, followed close behind carrying a bowl of corn.

"Janine," Aunt Shirley barked, "we about ready to eat or what?"

My mom smiled tightly at Aunt Shirley. It's not that they didn't get along...it's just my mother didn't take flak from anyone. Aunt Shirley included. Mom taught elementary school for thirty years at Granville Elementary. Take it from me, in order to teach elementary kids, you have to be a scrapper.

"Matt and Garrett are in the backyard," Mom said, "throwing a stick to Nala. They will be in shortly."

My brother, Matt, recently married my best friend, Paige. Their first big step into newlywed bliss was to get a puppy. And what a cute little pain-in-the-butt it was. Nala was a chow and lab mix. I called it a chab. Nala was hyperactive, chewed on everything, and was as cute as a button.

"Wellll," Aunt Shirley slurred slightly, "they better hurry. I'm about to starve to death."

"Simmer down there," Garrett called from the doorway. "I'd hate to have to arrest you for public intoxication."

"Nice try there, Ace. I may be slightly intox—toxi—drunk, but we ain't in public!"

Garrett's narrowed his eyes at her. "Public enough for me."

"Settle down you two," Mom chided. "This is supposed to be a nice family dinner."

I wrapped my arms around Garrett and pressed my lips against his ear. "Play nice. She's an old lady."

"I heard that you ninny!" Aunt Shirley bellowed.

Nala chose that moment to barrel around the corner and run straight into the dining table leg, causing her to curl up like a roly poly and do two somersaults across the hardwood floor.

"I've almost taught her to walk on all four legs," Matt joked as he walked into the room. "She's still so clumsy."

"What kind of wine would you like me to open for our dinner, Janine?" Doc asked my mom.

"Whatever kind goes with nuts," Aunt Shirley joked.

Mom gave Aunt Shirley her best teacher stare. She could still do it after all these years. Aunt Shirley grinned but didn't say anything else. Even Aunt Shirley knew where the line with my mom was.

Dinner was actually nice, considering Aunt Shirley continued to drink even more…which made her run her mouth even more. By the time dessert rolled around, we were all ready to gag her.

I'd just finished loading the last of the leftovers in the Falcon when Virginia Webber called me on my cell phone. I let out a victory whoop when she said she'd like to meet the next morning to go over the interview questions. I did a jig all the way back inside the house to tell everyone the good news.

"I'm goin' too." Aunt Shirley got up from the chair she was sitting in. She stood for about three seconds before she started swaying dangerously. A sure sign she's had too much to drink. "In fact, I should prolly jus' sleep over at your place tonight so's we can get a head start t'morrow."

I laughed at her ridiculous statement. "Virginia lives across the hall from you and down one apartment. You're literally twelve steps from her. There's no need to stay with me."

Aunt Shirley stuck out her lower lip like a pouty three year old. "You're no fun a'tall. I don't wanna go home alone. I wanna go with you."

Aunt Shirley's whining went straight to my head. I silently counted to five.

"I'm sorry," Paige whispered as she came to hug me goodbye. "Let me know how it goes."

A few minutes later I went into the kitchen to tell Mom and Doc good night. They were standing side-by-side at the kitchen sink washing dishes and murmuring. They immediately sobered when they saw me.

"We could hear her in here," Mom said. "Don't let her talk you into anything you don't want to do, Ryli Jo Sinclair."

In the end I decided to let Aunt Shirley stay over. Garrett followed me home and carried a passed out Aunt Shirley from the Falcon into my house. As he placed her on the bed she stirred from her tipsy stupor enough to give him what-for.

"Don't you be tryin' to sneak a peek at my goodies," Aunt Shirley said.

Garrett shuddered. "As if."

"Plenty of men have seen my goodies, and ain't a one of them complained."

I snickered at her ridiculous statement. "Aunt Shirley, do you need anything? A glass of water? Pain reliever?"

I figured she was gonna have a heck of a hangover tomorrow.

Miss Molly, my black and white longhaired cat, chose that moment to jump up on my bed to see what all the fuss was about. She gingerly made her way close to Aunt Shirley, her nose and whiskers twitching nonstop.

Aunt Shirley suddenly reached inside her mouth, yanked out her teeth, and shove them into Garrett's hand. "Watch over these for me, would ya, Ace?" She was snoring before her head hit the pillow.

Miss Molly arched her back, screeched, and raced out of the room.

Neither of us said a word. We simply watched in horror as rivulets of saliva dripped from the dentures in Garrett's hand.

"There's a glass next to the sink," I said. "Just fill it with water and drop the teeth in. Hand sanitizer is in the cabinet."

Garrett didn't say anything.

"Garrett, you okay?"

Garrett blinked a couple times, coming out of his stupor. He looked down at his hand and blanched, his face going pale. Without a word he slipped silently from the room, leaving me alone with a snoring Aunt Shirley. I was almost tempted to smother her with my pillow.

"You are an amazing woman," Garrett said a little while later, pulling the hide-away out from the couch for me to sleep on.

My house was only eight hundred square feet with one bedroom and bathroom. I really didn't have room for a sleepover guest. Miss Molly had been so traumatized by Aunt Shirley's behavior that she elected to sleep in the bathtub.

"Thanks." I tossed the pillow I didn't smother Aunt Shirley with onto the hideaway and laid down, patting the space beside me.

Garrett grinned. "Maybe for just a minute."

"Did you put enough hand sanitizer on? I don't want Aunt Shirley germs all over me."

Garrett made a face at me when I mentioned Aunt Shirley. But then he smiled. "Just my germs all over you."

CHAPTER 5

"Slow down," Aunt Shirley snapped as I pulled out of the newspaper parking lot and headed toward the Manor for our meeting with Virginia.

I smirked at her. "I'm going twenty miles an hour. Perhaps if you didn't still have a hangover, twenty wouldn't feel so rough."

Aunt Shirley shoved a huge pair of sunglasses on her face. They covered her eyes, half her forehead, and nearly all her cheeks. She looked ridiculous.

"How about you shut your mouth," Aunt Shirley snapped. "I don't have a hangover. I never get hangovers."

I snorted. I knew for a fact that was a lie. I could hardly keep her sober at Paige's bachelorette party. What I discovered is that Aunt Shirley doesn't need to be completely sober to catch a killer.

I really wasn't in the mood to spar with her, though. It was bad enough her little sleepover made me half an hour late at the office, but the fact Hank made me bring Aunt Shirley along to my interview just set wrong with me. I don't really care that he thinks people open up to her. I needed a little distance from Aunt Shirley right now. I was about at the end of my rope when it came to having to look after her.

Mindy had helped me brainstorm different questions and avenues for my big front-page story while Aunt Shirley drank a gallon of coffee and dozed half the morning. As I was getting ready to leave, Hank said that if I didn't submit an outline to him by the evening, my chance at the front-page cover would be over. I really needed this interview to work today.

34

"Run me through Burger Barn real quick," Aunt Shirley demanded. "I finally feel good enough to eat. I need to refuel on a big, greasy cheeseburger."

Our Burger Barn is a little different than other burger joints in that they sell breakfast, lunch, and dinner. When you are one of the only restaurants in town, it pays to serve all three meals.

Since it was one-thirty, the drive-thru line wasn't that long. Within five minutes I paid for the lunches, collected the burgers, and parked in the Burger Barn parking lot to scarf down the food.

"You haven't mentioned my new sunglasses," Aunt Shirley pouted after she wolfed down half of her cheeseburger. "Don't you like them?"

I sneaked a peek again as I bit into my cheeseburger. Still just as ridiculous. "They're awful big."

"You may not know this, but I've developed a few wrinkles lately."

More like a few hundred *wrinkles.*

Aunt Shirley pushed the glasses farther up her nose. "And these sunglasses help to give me a little coverage."

"They cover your whole face."

Aunt Shirley wiped her mouth with a wadded up napkin. "Like I said, it helps give me a little coverage."

"Try to be on your best behavior today," I said. "Virginia is going to talk a lot about loving her three husbands. Something I'm sure you can't even wrap your head around."

"Darn right I can't. I'd never marry one man...much less three!" Aunt Shirley finished off the last of her cheeseburger, stuffed the wrapper back into the bag, pulled down the visor, and smeared on a horrendous shade of red lipstick. Aunt Shirley was a firm believer that if you didn't have on lipstick then you were naked. "I ain't promising to be good, but I'll try not to roll my eyes too often when she mentions these lover boys of hers."

I sighed. It was the best I was going to get from her. "Don't ruin this for her or for me."

Aunt Shirley flipped the visor back up. "I won't. Even if I think it's stupid, I won't make fun of her."

I parked in the visitor's parking at the Manor and walked inside. Dozens of residents were milling about the large great room, reading, playing board games, and sitting in front of a fire. Valentine hearts with cute sayings were hanging down with fishing line from the ceiling.

"If it weren't for some of the people here, this would be a really nice place, Aunt Shirley. I don't know why you don't embrace it more."

"It's a place for old people," Aunt Shirley said. "I ain't old!"

Please, you and Methuselah were probably in diapers together.

We passed the cafeteria and headed toward Aunt Shirley's wing. I slowed when I saw Thomas Shifley and another orderly standing near the cafeteria doors looking over their shoulders. Shifley handed the other orderly something. I couldn't tell what it was, but it didn't seem very big. Almost like a piece of paper. The other guy didn't look at it, but stuck it in his pocket.

"I forgot to tell you," I said as I pushed the button for the elevator. "I overheard a conversation yesterday about the stolen boxes from the pantry."

Aunt Shirley perked up. "What did you hear?"

We walked into the elevator and Aunt Shirley pushed the button for her floor. Luckily we were alone because Aunt Shirley decided to pass gas.

"Jeez…really?"

Aunt Shirley laughed. "Tequila gets me every time!"

The elevator doors opened and I hurried into her deserted hallway, gasping for clean air.

"So," Aunt Shirley demanded, "what did you find out?"

I shot her an evil look and continued to breathe in the fresh air. "I learned that Sheri Daniels did in fact place the order, it arrived, and someone named Kaylee was the last person to see the boxes. Kaylee said she put the boxes in the pantry."

Aunt Shirley clucked her tongue. "That Kaylee Jones isn't exactly a rocket scientist. Ya get my meaning?"

I thought about the crying girl and her newborn baby she was trying to support. "I get your meaning."

"But I don't think there's anything sinister about Kaylee. Of course, I'm not even sure what was in the boxes, so who knows whether or not she'd need to steal them. Do you think it was medication?"

I shrugged. "I haven't heard anyone say what was in the boxes now that I think about it."

"If it was medication or something like that, then it could bring in money. I guess maybe Kaylee could have stolen it."

"Well, she did say she had a baby to feed," I conceded.

Aunt Shirley frowned. "I still think there's something more."

"And this is weird. Your neighbor, Ray Manning, was in there demanding to know if Sheri had reordered his stuff."

"What stuff?" Aunt Shirley asked.

I threw up my hands. "How would I know? He was just yelling about whether or not she'd placed the new order for him."

"I'm telling you that man is bad news."

I couldn't agree more.

I was about to knock on Virginia's front door when Lovey swung it open.

"Come in, come in," she gestured with her drink. "You came at just the right time. We're having cocktails."

At two o'clock on a Thursday afternoon?

Aunt Shirley knocked me aside, causing me to stumble into the wall. "I've never turned down a cocktail before."

I groaned and followed them inside.

CHAPTER 6

"I hope you don't mind," Virginia said, "but I've asked Lovey and Dotty to stay. We've been friends for about sixty years now, and they've been right there with me through the marriages and deaths of all my husbands. Better friends I couldn't ask for."

I gave Aunt Shirley a meaningful look. These were exactly the type of women she needed to be hanging around.

"Not at all," I said. "I think it's wonderful you guys all live on the same floor and right next door to each other. Aunt Shirley is lucky to have you guys for neighbors."

Aunt Shirley shot me a "get real" glare that I ignored. I was determined to enjoy myself with this interview and the ladies surrounding me. It would be a nice change of pace to be around actual nice old ladies.

Virginia's apartment was nothing like Aunt Shirley's. There was vibrant color everywhere. A lot of old Victorian-style Queen Anne furniture, collectable antiques, and myriad pictures adorned the walls.

I strolled over to look at family pictures. Some were of Virginia surrounded by what I assumed were her children and grandchildren. Others were of her at different stages of her life with different men. I assumed these were her husbands. In every picture Virginia was the image of perfection.

I turned and looked at Virginia standing with the other ladies by the bar. Even though she was probably in her seventies, she was still a strikingly beautiful woman with her platinum blond bob, prominent cheekbones, narrow nose, and full lips. Her body was still trim and fit, too.

She reminded me of Helen Mirren from the *Red* movies. I think Mirren is one of the most beautiful women in film today. And the fact she likes to play characters that are strong and can kick butt is a huge plus.

"Ryli," Lovey called over to me from the bar, "what would you like to drink?"

"Water is fine."

Silence.

"It's a cocktail party you ninny," Aunt Shirley snapped. "You can't have water. You have to have a drink."

I sighed. Obviously I was going to have to be a full participant in order to get what I wanted. "How about a beer?"

Silence again.

Aunt Shirley opened her mouth, no doubt to chew me out, but Virginia laid a hand on Aunt Shirley's arm. "How about an Old Fashioned, dear? It's one of my favorite drinks."

I shrugged. I had no idea what that even was. "Okay."

There were probably nine different types of hard liquor on the countertop, seltzer water, a shaker, and an assortment of small bottles called bitters in various flavors. Orange slices, maraschino cherries, olives, and tiny pearl onions were sitting in a white, compartmentalized serving tray.

These women obviously took their cocktails seriously.

"What is all this?" I asked.

"This," Virginia said primly, "is a dying art. Back in our day, cocktail parties were all the rage. Women didn't drink beer, we drank cocktails." She crushed up a sugar cube with the back of a spoon, added bitters to the sugar and mixed it together until it was a murky liquid. She then added a cherry and crushed it up in the glass before adding three ice cubes. Next came two ounces of bourbon, a quick stir, and a garnish of another cherry and a sliver of orange.

"Here you go…an Old Fashioned. Sure to cure what ails you. It's what I always drink." She handed me the diminutive drink. It looked and smelled strong enough to put hair on my chest.

"Shouldn't you put like a lot of seltzer in it to water it down?" I asked.

They all laughed at me. Obviously that was a ridiculous request to them.

"I'll take a Gin and Tonic," Lovey said.

"Manhattan for me," Dotty added.

Virginia turned to Aunt Shirley. "I've heard about how much you love your tequila, so might I suggest a Spanish Fashion?"

Aunt Shirley gasped. "That used to be my signature drink back in my cocktail party days. How did you know?"

Virginia smiled sweetly at Aunt Shirley. "Lucky guess. I'd say the drink suits you."

I peered over the shoulder of Lovey and watched as Virginia started mixing and pouring drinks.

"A Gin and Tonic is self-explanatory," I said. "And I've at least heard of a Manhattan. But what's a Spanish Fashion?"

"Heaven in a glass," Aunt Shirley sighed.

Virginia laughed. "It's a combination of tequila, sweet vermouth, bitters, and a maraschino cherry."

"At this rate, we're all going to be schnockered by two-thirty," I said.

Another round of laughter.

"Honey," Lovey said, "we've been having a daily cocktail since we were in our twenties. "

Once all the drinks were poured, Virginia invited us into her living room to start the interview. She held court sitting in a cream colored satin wing chair with ornate dark armrests and legs. Aunt Shirley and I sat on a smaller matching loveseat, and Lovey and Dotty sat across from us also in a matching loveseat. At least I think they call them loveseats. Maybe they were settees? This kind of fancy furniture always threw me off.

Lovey and Dotty were conservatively dressed, like Aunt Shirley, in slacks and flowery dress shirts with buttons down the front. Virginia was elegantly dressed in a yellow and cornflower blue knee-length dress, which brought out the blue in her eyes.

Everything about this woman screamed sophistication and poise.

"Where shall we begin, dear?" Virginia asked.

"Well, instead of jumping right in to your marriages," I said, trying not to notice the way she flinched, "how about we start with you three. Have you always known each other?"

"Lovey and I have," Dotty said, swirling her Manhattan. "Virginia moved to Granville when we were in elementary school. Around 1954 or '55, wasn't it?"

Virginia nodded. "Around there. My daddy was a lawyer, and he moved us from Kansas City to Granville to open his own practice."

"And you all became instant friends?" I asked. I tried to ignore the fact I could heard Aunt Shirley's ice clinking, signaling she was about done with her drink already.

Dotty and Lovey exchanged looks. I didn't know how to read it.

"Well, to be honest," Lovey said, "even before Virginia moved to town, Dotty and I had to keep our friendship on the down-low as you young people say. My daddy was the only doctor in town, while Dotty's dad was…"

Dotty smiled at Lovey. "You can say it." Dotty turned to me. "My daddy was the town drunk. When he came back from World War II, he was never quite the same."

My eyes filled with tears. I knew what she was saying. For a few years we lost Matt to survivor's guilt after he came back from his tours in Afghanistan. There's a lot more help and understanding of what PTS and survivor's guilt is today than there ever was for men coming back from wars years ago. In fact, if it wasn't for Garrett's friendship, understanding, and help, I don't know where Matt would be today.

"I'm sorry to hear that," I said kindly.

Dotty waved me off. "My dad died from liver failure when I was in seventh grade. My mom left with the first guy that came through town, and I was left alone."

"Omigosh!" I exclaimed.

Dotty smiled at Lovey. "Lovey came forward and told her parents about us being friends, and so they decided to take me in, raise me in their home. Meanwhile, Virginia's parents and Lovey's parents became fast friends, which meant we all got to hang out together. So naturally we've pretty much all three been inseparable throughout our lifetime."

Lovey took a sip of her drink. "Times were different in the early '60s when we graduated from high school. Most women got married, started a family, and stayed home to raise their babies. But after graduation Daddy let Dotty and me work at his doctor's office, while Virginia pretty much married Barry straight out of high school."

I perked up at the mention of the first husband.

"Barry," Virginia sighed. "I still miss him to this day."

"Before we start on Barry, could I have another drink?" Aunt Shirley asked.

"Of course," Dotty said. "I'll make it for you. I'm gonna need another drink too if we're going to talk about this. You guys go ahead and talk."

No time like the present. "So, tell me about Barry."

CHAPTER 7

Virginia got a faraway look in her eye and smiled. "Barry was seriously the love of my life. He was everything I ever wanted in a husband. He graduated with us, you see."

Lovey got up and retrieved a box of Kleenex, while Dotty came back with a refill for both her and Aunt Shirley.

"So before I tell my story, I want you to know that this time period spans over fifty years. While these stories may seem sad, please understand for me it's fifty years worth of memories and love. I have two wonderful children, and every one of these men loved me and I loved them."

I nodded and smiled at Virginia. "I understand. And that's exactly what I want for you. I want you to tell your love story this Valentine's Day."

"Thank you." Virginia dapped at the corner of one eye.

"So what happened with Barry?" Aunt Shirley demanded.

"What happened? I married him. And for a very short time we were deliriously happy. See, Barry contracted tuberculosis as a little boy, and he never fully recovered from it. There was no vaccination back then like there is today. One day he came home from work—he was working at my daddy's law office doing filing and legal paperwork for him—and he was very sick. To be honest, I wasn't overly worried at the time. He was almost always getting the flu or pneumonia or bronchitis." Virginia shrugged. "Unfortunately he just didn't recover. He was sick one day, gone the next. We called the doctor—Lovey's daddy—and he and the girls came right over. We'd only been married a little over a year." Virginia sighed and blew her nose. "Five months before my twentieth birthday, and I was already a widow." She grabbed another Kleenex out of the box and dabbed her eyes. "I really, really loved him."

Lovey soothingly patted Virginia's hand while Dotty went to fill Virginia's glass with another Old Fashioned.

"Yep," Lovey added, "Dotty and I stayed throughout the night, taking turns sitting with Barry. Unfortunately everything we did just wasn't enough. He died the next day."

"What did your dad think happened?" I asked Lovey. "Was there an autopsy done?"

Lovey shook her head. "Honey, again these were different times. Barry contracted tuberculosis when he was a child. He was lucky to still be alive. We all knew it was a matter of time before Barry got so sick he couldn't fully recover."

"And Lovey's right," Virginia added. "Even Barry's parents were surprised he lived as long as he did. A common cold could leave him incapacitated for weeks. There was extensive damage to his lungs from the TB."

"And your second husband?" Aunt Shirley prodded.

Virginia quickly looked down at the table, saying nothing for a few minutes. "Stanley really was a good man. He just took the coward's way out."

Aunt Shirley frowned. "I see. And what drove him to that?"

Drove him to what? I don't see anything.

"I honestly don't know." Virginia suddenly looked frail and sad beyond her years. "Let me start at the beginning. See, it took me years to get over Barry's death. I didn't remarry until many years later. I was probably twenty-six or so when I met Stanley. He was a prosecuting attorney in Brywood, and my daddy really liked him." Virginia smiled softly and took another drink of her Old Fashioned. "And Daddy was right. Stanley was everything I could hope for. Juries loved him because he was so personable. In the seven years we were married, I had two kids—Stanley Junior and Rachael. And he loved those kids. With all his heart he loved those kids."

"Cutest little things you ever saw," Lovey added. Her round cherub face flushed from the alcohol.

"Stanley loved his job and he loved pampering me and the kids. I can't remember once in the seven years we were married that he ever said a harsh word or yelled at either me or the kids. He loved us all so much."

"He sounds wonderful," I said. "What happened?"

Virginia swiped at her eyes. "I honestly don't know. My mom had been sick a few days earlier, so I told Stanley I wanted to visit her and daddy, and that the kids and I would be back Sunday night. My parents had moved to the country a few years before and were living in between Granville and Brywood. Stanley said that was fine. He had a trial on Monday he needed to prepare for. So I packed the car early Saturday morning and left. I talked with him briefly Saturday evening around four and everything was fine."

"You doing okay, Virginia?" Dotty asked gruffly. "We can take a break if you need."

Virginia shook her head. "No, I'm fine." She took a deep breath. "When the kids and I came home Sunday evening, I found him in his study. There were two empty bottles tipped over on his desk, and he'd shot himself in the head."

Whoa!

"And you never had a red flag or anything?" Aunt Shirley demanded.

"I swear to you, no." Virginia said.

"Neither did we," Lovey added. "He always seemed so happy with his life."

"So his death was ruled a suicide?" I asked gently.

Virginia nodded. "As much as I can't believe it, yes."

"And my God did those babies take it hard," Dotty said and took a drink. "They may have just been youngins, but they cried for months after their daddy was gone."

I picked up my Old Fashioned and swallowed past the lump in my throat. The burn of the liquor going down felt nice on my suddenly dry throat.

Virginia wiped her eyes with the wadded up tissue. "I know it will be hard to shy around his death in your article, but please know that the Stanley that shot himself was not the Stanley that we all knew and loved. I have no idea what suddenly drove him to take his own life."

"I'm not exactly sure how I'm going to write the article yet, but rest assured it will lift up the love you had and received from these men, not about their deaths."

Virginia wiped her eyes again. "Thank you. That means a lot."

"And your third husband?" I asked as gently as I could. "What about him?"

All three ladies laughed, breaking the somber mood.

"Oh boy," Lovey hooted, her cheeks jiggling with movement. "Where to start about him?"

"Bob was a partier. A good-time guy," Virginia said. "He loved food and drinking. I married him when I was in my fifties."

"I still miss his pasta primavera and cheesecake," Dotty sighed.

Virginia set her drink down on an end table next to her. "Bob was the manager of the produce department at the local grocery store here in Granville. That's how I met him. He was stacking apples, singing opera, and had such an air about him I was immediately drawn to him. Of course I'd seen him before—Granville is a small town with only one grocery store. I knew his wife had died years before and he was single, but I never had the nerve to approach him."

"He sounds larger-than-life," I said.

Virginia laughed. "He was actually. He was over six feet tall and weighed nearly three hundred pounds. Anyway, one thing led to another, and three months later I was married. He loved to entertain. He did most of the cooking in the house, which was fine by me." She sobered and shook her head. "We'd been married five years when he suddenly died of a heart attack at our annual Christmas party we held every year."

I gasped. "He died in front of your guests?"

Virginia nodded her head. "But understand, it's the way he would have wanted to go. Surrounded by his friends, his food and drink. The doctor had told us if Bob didn't lose weight, his heart would eventually give out."

Dotty swirled her drink slowly and methodically. "Went down right in the middle of your living room floor and pretty much died before he hit the ground. It was that sudden."

"So shocking," Lovey added.

"I miss those Christmas parties." Dotty downed the last of her cocktail.

Lovey nodded. "He sure was a good time." She broke out into a smile and nudged Virginia's knee. "This calls for another round. Let's have a drink and toast Bob."

I did my best to try and keep up with the number of drinks these ladies had consumed, but I'd lost track. Thankfully I was still nursing my first drink.

"I promise not to make this article depressing," I told Virginia as Dotty went to mix another round.

Virginia smiled. "Oh, honey, it's not depressing. Love is never depressing. I loved every one of these men differently, and every one of them holds a very special place in my heart. I put myself out there each time because I believed love would conquer all. I still believe that. Love should never be skirted away from…it should be whole-heartedly embraced. Even if it doesn't turn out like you thought it would, it's still better to have loved than not."

I looked at the clock. Aunt Shirley and I were going on two hours. Hank would be leaving the office around five, so I had less than an hour to draw up an outline for him. "I guess we should be going. I think I have everything."

"Nonsense." Lovey's flushed face grinned at me. "Surely you have time for one more drink!"

I suppressed a groan when Aunt Shirley jumped up from her chair and started heading to where Dotty was making more drinks.

I pulled out my phone and shot Hank a text telling him I got the story and I'd have the outline to him by seven o'clock.

Aunt Shirley and I ended up staying another hour drinking and telling stories. Well, they drank and told stories. I had plain tonic water and listened attentively. I wasn't about to have to text Garrett for a ride home.

By the time five o'clock rolled around and Aunt Shirley had finished off her last Spanish Fashion, I was about out of patience.

"Aside from all the death talk in the beginning," Aunt Shirley said as she shut Virginia's front door, "I haven't had this much fun in an afternoon since my phone got stuck on vibrate!"

CHAPTER 8

We didn't even make it across the hall to Aunt Shirley's apartment before she started in on not staying there. "Do you think you can run me by the grocery store real quick?"

"Why?"

"I need to pick up some soup. Soup is a good dinner when you have to eat all alone. And it looks like that's what I'll be doing tonight...eating all alone."

I shook my head and chuckled at her pathetic attempt at puppy-dog eyes. "I have soup at my house. You can eat dinner with me tonight then I'll bring you back. By the way, for a lady who just guzzled five drinks, you look and sound pretty sober."

Aunt Shirley looped her arms around mine as we walked toward the elevator. "What you have to understand about the cocktail party is that you drink to socialize. You don't drink to get drunk."

The elevator slid open and out walked Thomas Shifley, Ray Manning, and the other male orderly that Shifley handed the paper off to.

Manning shoved a handful of chocolate into his mouth. "Too old and feeble to walk on your own there, Shirley?"

Aunt Shirley withdrew her arms from mine and stood up straight and tall. "Watch it, Manning, or I'll shove those chocolates so far down your throat you won't have time to think about breathing."

Manning stopped laughing and pounded his cane on the floor. "Don't you talk to me like that, woman!"

Aunt Shirley grinned wickedly, her head and body doing a little sassy shake. "I hope you choke on those chocolate peanuts and die."

Manning pounded his cane again. "They're espresso beans, you stupid woman!"

"Well excuuuuuse me!" Aunt Shirley cackled. "I hope you choke on those chocolate covered espresso beans and die!"

I heard an apartment door open and saw Lovey, Dotty, and Virginia slowly make their way out into the hallway.

"Everything all right out here?" Lovey called.

Manning looked over at the three of them then back at us. "These two here just threatened me. You heard it right? Maybe you should call down to the desk and report it."

I sucked in my breath. One more report of disturbance and Aunt Shirley was out.

"We didn't hear anything of the sort," Lovey said as she crossed her arms over her chest. "And Thomas Shifley, if you or Carl Baker say otherwise, we'll testify we heard things the other way around. And while we're at it, Ray Manning...if you don't stop sending Virginia threatening letters, we'll make sure *you're* the one kicked out!"

"Yeah!" Virginia and Dotty echoed.

Carl Baker.

I now had a name to put with the face. I sized Carl Baker up and decided he didn't pose too much of a threat. He was a pretty puny looking man. Taller than Shifley, but not by much. And he had a rather unfortunate receding hairline.

Shifley held up his hands and took a step back. "I didn't hear nothing."

"Me either," Baker agreed.

Manning scowled at the orderlies. "You lily-livered fools. Grow a backbone!"

Thomas Shifley and Carl Baker both continued to back up toward the elevator. Shifley reached out and pushed the button to go down. The elevator immediately opened and both men fled inside.

"Looks like no one's got your back there, Manning," Aunt Shirley taunted.

"This isn't over!" Manning shoved a handful of chocolate covered espresso beans into his mouth and hobbled down the hallway toward his apartment.

I turned to Virginia. "What kind of letters is he sending you?"

Virginia's eyes filled with tears. "Just vague mean things about me, about my husbands. Even a couple about Lovey and Dotty."

My mouth hung open. "Have you shown these letters to anyone else?"

The girls all shook their heads.

"No," Lovey said. "We just burn them when Virginia gets them. We don't want Mr. Manning to have that kind of power over her."

I frowned. I wasn't sure that was the best solution to the problem.

"You girls have a good night," Lovey called out as the three of them retreated back into Virginia's apartment.

Aunt Shirley walked past me and pushed the elevator button. "You still think this is a nice place to live?"

"Outside of Manning, and Thomas Shifley, and Sheri Daniels? Yes, I do."

"Humph!"

We rode the elevator down in silence. I was going over the outline I planned on submitting to Hank tonight. After hearing Virginia's whole story, I knew the direction I wanted to go for the front-page story.

Aunt Shirley and I walked past the cafeteria where dinner was being served. I was about to suggest we just eat in the cafeteria when Sheri Daniels's office door flew open and she came barreling out.

"Move. I'm in a hurry."

I took a tiny step back. More from shock than anything else. "Sorry. We didn't know you were coming out."

She narrowed her eyes at me. "What are you waiting for? I said move."

Aunt Shirley nudged me in the ribs, "You heard her. Move out of the way. You know what they say…ugly before beauty!"

I couldn't help but chuckle. I decided to grow a backbone of my own. "So, Sheri, any comment on the record about the missing items—or should I say *stolen* items? I'm sure the *Granville Gazette* readers would be interested in knowing how incompetent you and your staff really are."

Sheri's face turned bright red. I was almost afraid I'd stepped over the line. She looked ready to deck me. Instead, she stepped within two inches of my face. "You print one false word, and I'll make sure your aunt leaves tonight!"

"Pshaw!" Aunt Shirley guffawed. "That ain't no threat. I'd love to leave this place. I say we go back and print something right now!"

Sheri grabbed me painfully by my elbow. The pain was immediate and fierce, and I'm not ashamed to say I momentarily lost focus. She obviously worked out a whole lot more than I did.

Sheri gave me a quick shake, her black glasses sliding down her nose. "I wouldn't recommend playing with fire."

"You're gonna want to let go of my niece," Aunt Shirley whispered. "Or this here dart is gonna go right through that arm."

My tunnel vision was clearing, and I realized Aunt Shirley had her parka open and she'd whipped out a dart from her mini blowgun she loved to carry around. She had the dart poised above Sheri's arm.

Sheri immediately let go of my arm and turned to Aunt Shirley. "You're on thin ice here. You better watch your step."

I grabbed Aunt Shirley's parka sleeve and propelled her out the front door. I ran to the Falcon and got in, my heart still racing.

"These people are seriously whacked," I said.

"I've been trying to tell you. I don't know how I've survived living here all this time."

I looked over at Aunt Shirley, all snuggled up in her camo parka coat she loved to wear. I didn't see the dart anymore. "Where exactly do you have the dart and blowgun?"

Aunt Shirley grinned and spread open her coat. Inside were two tiny elastic loops. One loop held the blowgun, the other held the dart. She was always prepared.

I took Aunt Shirley back to my place. I knew Garrett was due for dinner around six, and I dreaded him finding Aunt Shirley there. Plus I still needed to get an outline to Hank.

I put Aunt Shirley in charge of heating up soup, grabbed my laptop and started plunking away. Miss Molly meowed and jumped up on the sofa with me. I gave her a few scratches before turning my focus back to the outline.

By the time I hit submit, the soup was ready to eat and the frozen garlic bread was buzzing in the oven. I looked at the clock on my phone and realized Garrett was due any minute.

Usually Garrett just let himself in, but I didn't want to surprise him with Aunt Shirley. I flipped on the front-porch light and hoped he was in a good mood. I didn't have to wait long before he arrived right on time.

"Why's she here?" Garrett asked as he stepped through the front door.

Aunt Shirley placed the bread on the table. "Hello to you, too. I just slaved over a hot meal, so don't give me grief."

I held in a sigh and walked over to Garrett. I slid my arms around him and laid my head on his chest. He took pity on me and wrapped his strong arms around me. "Should I ask what's going on, or give it a little while?"

I chuckled. "Give it a little while. Aunt Shirley needs to stay here at least through dinner. I can probably drop her off later and we can be alone."

Garrett leaned down and kissed me. "Holding you to that promise."

"You two love birds get over here and eat before I puke in my soup bowl. I swear, some things just can't be unseen."

I closed my eyes and prayed for patience. "She's definitely going home tonight. Promise."

Garrett ran his hand over my cheek. "I'll do you a favor and take her home for you."

"Deal. And I promise to make it up to you."

Garrett's eyes turned dark. "Deal."

"I'm right here you two," Aunt Shirley grumbled as she shoved a spoonful of soup in her mouth.

CHAPTER 9

"It's a decent article." Hank yanked his unlit cigar out of his mouth and walked out of his office toward Mindy, Aunt Shirley, and me. "You got your front-page story."

Mindy squealed and gave me a high five. "I knew it! Everyone loves a good love story, especially around Valentine's Day."

I preened. "That's what I was banking on."

"Let's not go patting ourselves too hard on the back," Hank said. "I'd rather have a murder, robbery, or even a good car chase instead. But this will have to do."

I bit back a grin. That would be as close as I'd ever get to an outright compliment.

"I still say there's a story with the missing boxes and burglaries over at the Manor," Aunt Shirley grumbled.

"You may be right," I conceded. "Sheri Daniels sure seemed upset over a few items. Makes me think there must have been something pretty important in the last shipment she ordered. So maybe there really is a story here."

"What kind of story?" Hank demanded.

I took a sip of my herbal tea—a Mindy special. "I didn't think much about it at first, since it's just some boxes from the Manor and a few personal items from the residents missing. But yesterday when I threatened to expose the story, Sheri Daniels went ballistic."

"Like how ballistic?" Hank said, his eyes lighting up.

"Like I had to put a dart to her arm and tell her to let go of Ryli…that ballistic," Aunt Shirley supplied.

"No kidding," Hank said sounding impressed. I wasn't sure if it was because Sheri wanted to protect her story that much or because Aunt Shirley held a dart to Sheri's arm.

"So I'm thinking there might be a story there after all," I said. "The only thing is, she threatened to kick Aunt Shirley out of the Manor if I ran with it."

"And?" Hank demanded. "What's the holdup?"

"Hank!" Mindy admonished. "Obviously it could mean Aunt Shirley loses her place to stay."

Hank yanked the cigar out of his mouth and pointed it at me. "We don't negotiate with terrorists! I don't care if it does mean the old lady's out on her butt. Get me the story if there's a story!"

"Fine," I said smugly. "Then Aunt Shirley can come live with you when she gets kicked out."

Hank's face turned purple. I could see I hit a nerve. "Just get me that story, Sinclair. You hear me?"

"I hear you," I grumbled.

Hank turned on his heel, walked back into his office, and slammed the door. One of these days that door was gonna splinter into a thousand pieces from the amount of abuse it takes.

"So what's on your agenda tonight?" Mindy said, oblivious to the fact her husband was clearly insane.

"After work I'm taking Aunt Shirley home. Then I'm going home to take a bubble bath and get prettied up. I have a date with Garrett tonight." I looked pointedly at Aunt Shirley.

Aunt Shirley ignored me and continued filing her nails. "I ain't got much planned. I may play some cards with some friends."

Wait...what?

"Since when do you have friends?" I asked.

Aunt Shirley huffed. "I got friends. You don't know everything about me. After your boyfriend kicked me to the curb last night outside of the Manor so he could get hanky-panky from you, I picked myself up off the sidewalk and hobbled inside."

I rolled my eyes at her.

"There were some nice people inside playing cards and they offered to let me play with them tonight. So I am."

"That's wonderful," Mindy gushed. "See, making friends isn't so hard."

I suddenly had a very bad feeling.

* * *

I dropped Aunt Shirley off at the Manor around four with a promise she'd behave and headed home. I had an hour and a half to soak, primp, and be out to Garrett's for dinner.

I unlocked my front door and was greeted by Miss Molly. By the way she was shrieking, she obviously thought she was starving. I opened a small can of flaked salmon and mixed in a couple tablespoons of dry cat food.

I opened a bottle of Riesling and poured a small glass, carrying it into the bathroom. I lit a vanilla lavender candle, dispensed a capful of vanilla lavender bubble bath into the running water, and went to pick out something to wear.

I decided on a pair of black leggings, silver tank top, a long-sleeved black and silver cardigan sweater, and my black boots.

I piled my hair on top of my head, opened Pandora on my phone, and hurried back into the bathroom. Turning off the water I slid down into the hot, steamy water and sighed. The smell of vanilla lavender immediately soothed me. I closed my eyes and let my mind drift.

I heard my cell phone announce a text. I sent up a quick prayer that it wasn't from Aunt Shirley demanding I come pick her up. I wiped my hands on a towel and grabbed my phone. I smiled when I saw the text from Paige.

Just wanted to say have fun tonight. I know you've been stuck with Aunt Shirley the last few days. Talk later. I'm off to make a baby!

I chuckled and drained the tub, toweled off, and quickly got dressed. I brushed my hair and gave it a quick curl at the ends. I was ready to go with a few minutes to spare.

I'd recently splurged on a slate colored parka that was filled with goose down and had a faux fur brim. It was expensive, but worth it since it kept me warm in the cold Missouri winter.

I threw a kiss to Miss Molly, grabbed my phone, and hopped in the Falcon. Garrett's house is out in the country, about five miles from town. He has seven acres, including a one-acre pond behind the house.

His road had recently been plowed to remove the snow, but I still made sure to go extra slow. The Falcon wasn't exactly a great winter car.

I parked in his circle drive and made my way up the cobblestone walkway. Garrett opened the door before I even reached the front porch.

"A little early," he said and gave me a kiss on my lips. "That's always a good sign."

I laughed and pushed past him, hurrying into the warm house. I hung my jacket up on the peg by the door. "I know we haven't had a lot of snow this winter, but I wish it would ease up on the cold temperatures."

"It's called winter for a reason, Ryli," Garrett said dryly.

I stuck my tongue out at him and followed him into the dining room. The food was already laid out. He had a battery-operated candle burning at the far end of the table and an opened bottle of wine between our plates.

"Wow, everything looks amazing." I narrowed my eyes at him. "What's going on?"

Garrett laughed. "Nothing. I swear. I just wanted to have a nice meal tonight. I feel like we're constantly bypassing each other."

"You realize you still have to do something special next week for Valentine's Day, right?"

Garrett threw back his head and laughed. "Yes. Now sit down and let's eat."

He'd prepared baked chicken, jasmine rice, and steamed asparagus with a bottle of Scully's White. Scully's was a local Missouri wine from Cellar Ridge Winery. He picked up the bottle and started to pour me a glass. "What's wrong? I can tell by the look on your face you're thinking about something."

I smiled. "I just don't understand how you found time to do all this after you've worked all day."

Truth is I'm terrified that if things get any more serious between us, I'll not be able to measure up to what Garrett expects.

63

Garrett served in the military, embraces structure, has an actual career, and pretty much has life whipped into shape. I'm lucky to remember to feed Miss Molly in the mornings. I still pick my clothes up off the floor and sniff them to make sure they don't stink before I put them on. I couldn't imagine being able to get home from work and throw something like this together. There's a reason why I have soup every night for dinner at my house.

"Ryli, I enjoy doing this. It's how I relax. Don't start measuring what I do by what you do, okay. Let's just enjoy."

"You're right." I gave him a cheeky grin. "After all, you've had *years* more practice at this than I have."

I could tell by the twitch of his lips he wanted to smile. "Watch it."

I laughed and allowed myself to relax and enjoy the meal. I've been worrying more and more lately about where our relationship was going. We've been seeing each other about four months now, and I'm perfectly content with where things stand with us. But I also know Garrett will be forty in a couple years, and he's already hinted about me moving in. When I think of the next logical step, the spit in my mouth dries up.

After dinner I carried the dirty dishes into the kitchen and stacked them in the dishwasher while he put the leftovers in the refrigerator. He topped off my glass of wine and we went into the living room to cuddle on the couch.

"So tell me about your week." He draped his arm behind me over the couch as I snuggled as close to him as possible.

"Remember I told you I was doing that interview with Virginia Webber and the life she spent with her three deceased husbands? It was actually quite fun." I laughed at the look on his

64

face. "Simmer down policeman. It was fun because I learned about the importance of cocktail parties and making drinks like a Spanish Fashion. I also learned you never know how much time you have in life, so you better grab and love the person you're with because you never know."

"The first part sounds fun, if not a little scary. And the second part sounds like very good advice." He took my wine glass, set it on the coffee table, gathered me in his arms, and kissed me deeply. He ran his hands through my hair, causing me to shudder. I leaned my head back to give him better access to my neck…when my phone started ringing.

"Ignore it!" we both shouted at the same time.

After three rings it went to voicemail. A few seconds later it rang again.

"No, no, no," I whispered against his lips.

Garrett sighed and gave me a quick, hard kiss. "Might as well answer it. They're obviously gonna keep calling until you do."

I yanked the phone out of my cardigan sweater. I didn't recognize the local number. I slid my finger forcefully over the button. "What? For the love of God, *what* do you want?"

There was a moment of silence.

"Ryli Sinclair?" the female caller asked.

"Yes. Yes, it is. And no I don't want to buy anything. No I don't want to take a survey, and yes take me off your calling list."

I yanked the phone from my ear and was about to press the end button when I heard, "Ms. Sinclair, this is Oak Grove Manor. We have your aunt here, and you need to come pick her up immediately."

I sighed and put the phone back up to my ear. Garrett gave me a sympathetic smile. Obviously our night was going to come to an abrupt halt.

"Ms. Sinclair, are you there?"

I sighed again extra loud for the benefit of the caller. "Yes, I'm here. What's going on?"

"Well, if you wouldn't mind coming to the Manor to pick up your aunt I will explain when you get here."

"Why do I have to come get her? She lives there."

Silence.

"Ma'am," the caller huffed, "are you coming to get her or do we need to call the police?"

It was on the tip of my tongue to tell the snotty woman that I was in the presence of the police right now, but I didn't think that would win any points for Aunt Shirley.

"I'll be there in ten minutes," I said.

I hung up the phone without waiting for an answer.

"Doesn't sound good," Garrett mused.

"Nope," I sighed.

I was terrified what this meant. Were they kicking Aunt Shirley out of the Manor and she had to come live with me? I wasn't sure my mental health could take Aunt Shirley as a roommate.

"Wanna come with me?" I asked hopefully.

"Not on your life, babe." Garrett leaned over and kissed my nose. "You better go. Give me a call later and let me know what's going on."

I shuffled over to where my coat was hung and slowly zipped it around me. I was trying to prolong the inevitable as much as possible.

"Drive safe."

I swallowed past the lump in my throat. "I will. I'll text you later to let you know what's going on."

Garrett smiled and opened the door for me. "Try not to act like you're going to your death."

"It's how I'm feeling."

CHAPTER 10

Oak Grove Manor was lit up like a Christmas tree when I came to a screeching halt outside the front entranceway. I didn't even bother with parking the Falcon in the visitor's section. I dared them to tow me.

I yanked open the front door and marched to the information desk. Aunt Shirley was standing there looking as proud as a peacock. A lady I'd never seen before was standing next to her, along with Thomas Shifley and Sheri Daniels. I groaned. This was so not good. It didn't look like Aunt Shirley would be talking her way out of this one.

There were about eight elderly people milling around the large living area. Some were playing checkers, others reading by the fireplace. They looked perfectly happy to be there. For the hundredth time I wondered why Aunt Shirley couldn't be one of them.

"Ms. Sinclair, my name is Lucy Stevenson. I am the Executive Director for Oak Grove Manor." Her brown hair was cut in a classic bob, her wrinkle-free tailored suit fit perfectly against her body, and her black square glasses left no doubt she was all business. Even her handshake was crushing. I tried not to cringe so I wouldn't show weakness. "Let me get straight to the point. Your aunt was caught tonight playing strip poker with three gentlemen."

My mouth dropped open. Aunt Shirley grinned and nodded vigorously at me. Her top dentures bobbed up and down. She looked maniacal.

Lucy Stevenson cleared her throat. "This is a family-friendly facility. We pride ourselves on emphasizing the family part. We can't have this kind of behavior at our place."

Sheri Daniels and Thomas Shifley were both smirking at me.

"Where are the men?" I demanded. "I don't see them? Are they being kicked out?"

Lucy Stevenson sighed and shook her head. "This was their first offense. This is your aunt's tenth…in just this week. I've spoken to both our Coordinator, Sheri Daniels, and Mr. Shifley, the orderly for your aunt's floor, and they both assure me this week alone there have been many violations with regard to your aunt."

I glanced over at Aunt Shirley. She didn't even look guilty at the mention of all her violations. I didn't know whether to laugh or cry or scream.

"So what's your bottom line here, lady?" I demanded. At this point I couldn't even pretend to be polite.

Lucy Stevenson pursed her lips together tightly. "We are temporarily suspending your aunt from the Manor. She will need to be out of here by the weekend. I will have a hearing to determine her fate by the end of the month."

"It's Friday night for the love of God!" I cried. "How can I have her out by the weekend?"

Panicked, Lucy Stevenson quickly looked around the room at the other residents. "Please keep your voice down, Ms. Sinclair. I do not wish to disturb the other residents with this unpleasantness."

"Of course not. Just me, right?" I was practically yelling at this point, but I didn't care. "You only wish to ruin not only my night—but my life!"

"Oh suck it up, buttercup," Aunt Shirley said. "It ain't gonna be that bad."

A sudden sharp pain sliced through my right orbital and I knew it was only a matter of time before a full-fledged migraine came on. I rubbed my temple and admitted defeat. I knew when I was licked.

"Let's go get some of your stuff, Aunt Shirley. I'll take you to my place tonight." I scowled at Lucy Stevenson. "But this isn't over."

"Hot dog," Aunt Shirley hooted. "I'm breaking free!"

I rolled my eyes and started to walk away...all the while giving Sheri and Shifley my best squinty evil eye. The smirk on their faces told me I wasn't fazing them in the least.

I didn't say anything to Aunt Shirley until we got in the elevator. "What were you thinking?"

"What?" Aunt Shirley said. "We started out just playing poker, but I was getting bored fast."

My mouth dropped open. "Are you telling me strip poker was *your* idea?"

"Yep. Figured that would liven up the party. Old Man Jenkins was all for it!"

I closed my eyes and counted to ten. The elevator opened onto Aunt Shirley's floor. "How'd you get caught?"

Aunt Shirley's grin fell. "That loser Shifty caught us. Ray Manning had been over twice pounding on the door complaining of the noise, saying we were making him sick. I guess he got Shifty involved and Shifty found us."

"Please tell me you were dressed when you answered the door."

Aunt Shirley grinned. "I've always thought deep down Shifty wanted to see me naked. So I gave him that opportunity!"

Her laugh echoed loudly in the empty hallway.

I couldn't help but join in as we walked into her apartment. "Serves him right."

"You should have seen the look on his face. Like he swallowed a whole bag of lemons."

A card table and folding chairs were set up in the living room of Aunt Shirley's apartment. "Well, you have plenty of space for a card party."

"That's why we met in my apartment. Their apartments are cluttered and man gross. Mine was nice and empty."

"Go ahead and grab some things you'll need," I said. "I'll start picking up some of this trash."

Aunt Shirley did a little jig in the living room. "This is gonna be awesome. You and me living together. Think of the fun we'll have!"

She bolted out of the room before I could respond. I grabbed a trash bag from under the sink and started throwing away the garbage. I counted a half-eaten package of gummy bears, three empty water bottles, two empty bottles of Ensure, and an empty package of chewy chocolate chip cookies.

"What, no booze?" I hollered back to Aunt Shirley.

"Those weaklings! They said if they drank after five it keeps them up all night with heartburn and gas."

I kicked myself for asking.

I'd just thrown away the last of the trash when Aunt Shirley came back into the living room rolling a medium sized suitcase and carrying an even larger matching makeup bag.

It was on the tip of my tongue to tell her she wasn't staying that long. But then I realized I had no idea how long she really was staying.

"I'll see if I can't get Matt and Garrett to help get some of your things tomorrow." I opened Aunt Shirley's front door to leave. "Luckily we won't have to worry about your larger items for a few more weeks."

"You can burn it for all I care. I ain't never coming back so I don't need it."

The door across the hall opened and Lovey stepped out of her apartment. "What's going on? Phyllis Kregle down on first floor said she heard that your aunt was kicked out."

"You heard right!" Aunt Shirley pushed me aside with her suitcase. "I'm blowing this lame joint."

An elderly couple shuffled out of the apartment on the other side of Virginia. I'd never seen them before. I guessed them to be in their late seventies. They were both gray and thin, but the man towered over the woman by a good foot.

"We heard you are leaving us," the elderly lady said as they slowly made their way toward us.

"Jeez, word travels fast around here," I mumbled.

"We're the McElroys," he said. "Been here about four years now."

"I can't believe they really kicked you out," Dotty said.

Time to put a stop to the rumor mill. "It's just temporary."

"Nope," Aunt Shirley corrected me. "They told me I had the weekend to get out!"

Manning's door flew opened and he hobbled out into the hallway clutching a bag of chocolate covered espresso beans. "Best news I've heard all year! About time they kicked you out." He wiped sweat off his brow and swayed heavily on his cane.

"Now Mr. Manning," Mrs. McElroy scolded, "there's no need to be rude."

"You okay there, Mr. Manning?" I asked. He looked pale and weak.

"No I ain't okay. Your aunt's noise from her party has given me an upset stomach."

Aunt Shirley laughed. "You got the squirts because of my party? Doubt that."

He banged his cane on the floor. "It's true I tell you. I've been sick all day."

"You do look pretty pale there Mr. Manning," Lovey agreed. "What ails you?"

"Well, if you busybodies must know, I got the shakes, I'm vomiting, and I can't keep anything inside me."

Aunt Shirley rolled her eyes. "It sounds like you got the flu you idiot. If we're all lucky it'll kill ya!"

"Just go away so I can have some peace and quiet!" He turned on his heel, staggered back inside, and slammed the door closed.

"He doesn't look too good," Mrs. McElroy said. "Should we call someone downstairs to come take a look at him?"

"Nah, he'll be fine tomorrow." Aunt Shirley picked up her makeup bag. "Let's go driver."

"Shouldn't you say goodbye to Virginia?" I said.

"Virginia isn't in tonight," Lovey said. "She had a date with Bert Livingston."

"No way!" Aunt Shirley exclaimed and set her bag back down. "He's the most eligible bachelor at the Manor. That's some serious game right there."

"He asked her last week," Dotty said gruffly. "But she said no. Then after your visit, Ryli, she changed her mind. Guess maybe she's ready to get back out there again."

Tears filled my eyes. "I'm so happy for her. She's such a lovely lady. She deserves some happiness."

"Let's go home." Aunt Shirley picked up her makeup bag and rolled her suitcase down the hall. I shuddered at the thought of my home now being her home.

CHAPTER 11

"I don't understand why I have to be the one to keep her," I whispered into the phone. "I mean I'm sleeping on the couch in my own home!"

Mom was on the other end, trying to pawn Aunt Shirley off on me. Not the way I wanted to start my Saturday morning. I hadn't even had my coffee yet.

"I promise it will only be for a little while," Mom said. "I'll call Lucy Stevenson today. Her aunt and I are good friends, so maybe I can plead my case. If that doesn't work, we'll make Garrett use his pull and keep her there. But it may take a day or two."

"That all sounds good, but what about getting her out of the Manor today?"

Mom paused. "What's on your agenda this morning?"

I rolled my eyes, even though she couldn't see. "Well, Aunt Shirley's in the bathroom getting ready. She just informed me she had to be at Legends Salon & Nails in half an hour to get her hair done. Whatever that means."

Mom chuckled. "Just be glad all that Kool-Aid color washed out from Paige and Matt's wedding. I still don't know what possessed her."

Aunt Shirley had recently seen a young girl with multi-colored hair and decided she wanted that look for herself. Unfortunately it was a day before Paige was due to get married. We all still shake our head at Paige and Matt's wedding photos that feature Aunt Shirley, aka Rainbow Brite.

"That's true. It took quite a while for that to all wash out. I guess after we finish at Legends I'll go dumpster diving for some boxes outside the grocery store then run her by the Manor. At least go through the motions of packing some of her stuff."

"Good idea," Mom said. "Hopefully by then Garrett and I can figure something out."

"Please do, Mom. I don't know if I can stand her living here for very long."

"No worries, honey. I'll talk with you later."

I hung up the phone and texted Paige to tell her we'd meet her at Legends. No way was I doing Legends alone. I'd only been in there once since Iris died back in October. Died being my nice word for brutally murdered. Since then Legends has been taken over by Daphnie Dowerson. And trust me, she's as whacky as her name sounds. Which was another reason I was worried about Aunt Shirley going to see her. She could come out looking worse than she went in. Daphnie was known for her crazy cuts and colors. She was trained in some cutting-edge salon in Kansas City, so everyone in small town Granville flocked to her. I thought her cuts were ridiculous looking.

Aunt Shirley came scurrying into the living room, her purple polyester pants rubbing together so quickly I was afraid she'd catch fire. She yanked up her oversized bright pink patent-leather purse from the kitchen table. "Let's go. I need to have time to hear all the good gossip before I go under the dryer."

I shuddered at her purple and pink color combo.

"Wait. Why do you need to go under the dryer?" I asked.

"It's a surprise. Let's go!"

76

I barely suppressed a groan as I grabbed my purse and coat and followed her out the door and started up the Falcon. It was a frigid ten degrees outside, but at least no new snow.

It only took a couple minutes to get to Legends, park, and walk inside. There were two people sitting along the bench against the wall waiting their turn while Daphnie and Cindy Troyer already had customers in their chairs. Holly Parker, the new nail technician that took over when Iris died, was busy buffing and yacking away with her customer.

"Be right with you," Daphnie called out.

I absolutely hated coming into this shop. The ladies that usually came here were just a bunch of gossipers—Aunt Shirley included. I hung up our coats and led Aunt Shirley to one of the empty chairs in the waiting area. Hopefully Daphnie would be done soon and I could escape. Not that going to the Manor afterward was going to be any better.

I picked up an old *Cosmo* and half-heartedly flipped through. Not that I had any interest in what they said about how to keep a man, which every article seemed to be about. I nearly wept with joy when Paige walked through the door.

"Sorry I'm late," Paige said as she hung up her coat.

Aunt Shirley looked up from her hairstyle magazine and gave Paige the hawk eye, looking her up and down. "You don't look knocked up yet. What's taking so long?"

I grabbed hold of Paige's hand to keep her from going all spider monkey on Aunt Shirley. "You're not late, Paige. Come sit next to me."

Luckily Daphnie came over to get Aunt Shirley and we were left in peace. I tried not to look worried when Aunt Shirley started waving her hands above her head and Daphnie clapped her hands in glee. Something told me none of it was a good sign.

Daphnie plunked Aunt Shirley down in the chair and snapped a black cape on her. I was blocked from seeing anything else being done to Aunt Shirley.

"I'll go with you today to the Manor and pack some of her things," Paige said. "That's why I was late. I went ahead and stopped at the grocery store to pick up boxes for you. I have boxes, newspaper, and packing tape."

"Wow, you're seriously prepared. Which scares me. You realize I'm not taking her that long, right?"

"Of course, of course!"

I could tell Paige wasn't really sure.

"I'm *not*," I insisted. "The Manor *has* to take her back…or I'll go crazy." I was practically sobbing now. While I love Aunt Shirley, I didn't think I could take living with her full time.

"Your mom called Matt this morning and asked him to tag along with Garrett to talk with Lucy Stevenson. She thinks the two of them can sweet talk her into taking Aunt Shirley back."

I sent up a quick prayer that she was right.

"I just popped your aunt under the dryer and she'll be ready soon," Daphnie called out as she motioned for another customer to sit in her now-empty chair.

"I told my mom I'd run by the farm real quick this morning," Paige said. "I'll meet you at the Manor."

"Sounds good," I said. "I better go see if Aunt Shirley needs anything."

Aunt Shirley was sitting under a huge dryer next to another elderly lady. It was obvious from the forward tilt of Aunt Shirley's head that the heat from the dryer had already put her to sleep. She actually looked pretty peaceful with her hands folded in her lap, eyes closed, mouth slightly open.

I reached down to touch her when she suddenly let out a huge snore. Unfortunately, her top dentures chose that moment to pop out of her mouth and land in her folded hands. I shrieked and practically fell backward, causing me to wake Aunt Shirley.

"Oops." Aunt Shirley laughed when she saw her teeth in her hands. She picked them up and shoved them back in her mouth. "See, right as rain."

The little old lady sitting under the dryer next to Aunt Shirley nodded her head, which caused her rollers to clink against the side. "Yep, happens to me all the time."

"You know what I think?" Aunt Shirley said as we pulled into the visitor's space outside the Manor. "I think you're just jealous!" She got out her phone, took a selfie, and posted it to her two social media accounts.

I shut off the Falcon and turned to stare at her. Her new haircut was an absolute disaster. Think weed eater meets teenage emo angst. Her thin hair was now parted at her left ear and swept all the way over, causing her right eye to be partially hidden behind a cap full of white hair—hence the teenage emo angst part. Where her hair should have been on the left side of her head by her ear was now completely shaved, with just tiny stubble dotting her head—hence the weed eater part. But the absolute *best* part of the cut was the stubble. It was colored bright purple. Yes, bright purple. Then when you traveled back to the right side of her head—it was miraculously a head full of white hair again.

"It's the latest thing," Aunt Shirley assured me. "I feel like a new woman. I bet when the guys see me they're gonna be all over me. Maybe even Bert Livingston will dump Virginia and take me out. I'd make a good trophy wife."

I laughed at that. One thing for sure, Aunt Shirley could always make me laugh. "Let's go, Diva. Your audience awaits."

"Now you're catching on."

We met up with Paige at the front entrance. She took one look at Aunt Shirley's hair and her mouth hit the floor.

"I know," I said. "I had the same reaction."

Aunt Shirley held up a hand. "Daphnie says it's all the rage."

Luckily no one was manning the desk, so we were able to slide by without notice. Well, as much as three ladies—one sporting purple emo hair carrying boxes, newspaper, and tape—could go unnoticed.

As we got ready to pass Sheri Daniels's office, I pressed my finger to my lips letting them know to be quiet. Since the door was partially opened again, I couldn't stop myself from pressing my ear against the open space. By this time I was good at guessing voices.

"What do you mean he's not answering the door?" Sheri demanded. "I have the shipment he's been hounding me about."

"I'm telling you," Thomas Shifley said. "I tried twice to get him to open up, but he's not opening."

"On your next round you go up there and open that door. I want the money for his stuff!"

I motioned the girls to go and we scurried to the elevator. No one said a word as we waited for the elevator doors to open.

"So, what do you think?" Aunt Shirley demanded once the doors closed. "Think they were talking about Manning?"

"Sure do," I said. "Guess he's sicker than we all thought."

There wasn't anyone in the hallway when we got off the elevator, which wasn't unusual up on the third floor, but it still felt eerily quiet as Aunt Shirley unlocked her front door.

"You take the bedroom, and we'll start in the kitchen," I told Aunt Shirley. "We'll just take perishables that you will need for the next couple days until we know what's going on."

"I don't need much now that I'm living with you, roomie." Aunt Shirley said gleefully. "And don't forget to pack all my cans of black beans. I need to stay regular, ya know!"

I slowly closed my eyes and counted to ten. I couldn't imagine sitting at a dinner table night after night with Aunt Shirley and her plate of black beans. Garrett had better come through with keeping Aunt Shirley here or I was moving in with him—proper etiquette aside.

"Should you call your mom and see how things are going on her and Garrett's end?" Paige asked as she handed me a half-opened bottle of tequila from the freezer.

"Is this for me to drink or pack?" I joked. Even though I wasn't in much of a joking mood.

Bam! Bam! Bam!

"Manning, open up. I have your order here and you need to pay this invoice."

Aunt Shirley hobbled back in the kitchen. "Shifty's making enough noise to wake the dead."

I gave Aunt Shirley a sly grin. "I say we go over there and pay our last respects one more time before you leave."

Aunt Shirley ran to the door and flung it wide open. "What's going on here, Shifty?"

Thomas Shifley whirled and glared at Aunt Shirley. "None of your business. Aren't you supposed to be moved out?"

I stepped out in the hallway, Paige followed on my heels.

"You might wanna watch your tone," I said. "I've seen Aunt Shirley beat a man to death for less."

I hadn't really, but it sounded cool.

Aunt Shirley hooted and hit me in my arm.

Ouch!

"Good one." Aunt Shirley folded her arms across her sagging chest. "Yeah, Shifty. I once shot a man in Reno just to watch him die."

I bit back a chuckle. Paige couldn't help it and giggled. Aunt Shirley was good at deadpan deliveries.

"I don't know about no man getting shot in Reno," Shifley said, oblivious to the joke. "But what I do know is that this doesn't concern you, so get back in your apartment."

Virginia's apartment door opened. "My goodness, what's going on out here? I can hear you clear back in my bedroom."

"Whoohoo," Aunt Shirley danced. "You got Livingston tied up back in your bedroom you say?"

Virginia's elegant face turned pink. "Of course not! I just simply asked what was going on out here."

Three more front doors opened. Lovey and Dotty came into the hallway, each carrying a glass of water...or gin and tonic. I couldn't tell. And with them you never knew.

The McElroys also stepped out into the hallway from their apartment, muttering about the noise. An elderly female neighbor—apartment 370 on the other side of Manning—also wheeled her walker out into the hallway. The only resident on the floor not out in the hallway was Manning.

Something was definitely wrong.

"I do believe something is rotten in the state of Denmark," Aunt Shirley said.

Thomas Shifley gave us all one more scowl before he took a set of keys out of his pocket and unlocked Manning's front door. He cupped his hand around his mouth. "Ray Manning, you in here?"

Silence.

"Well, what're you waiting for?" Aunt Shirley demanded. "Get on in there and see what's going on."

Shifley was caught. He looked terrified, but he didn't want to let on he was. He wiped his hands on his uniformed white pants and pushed out a deep breath. He took one step into the apartment, and we all followed close on his heels.

"Ray Manning, are you in here?" Shifley called out again as he made his way slowly to the living room.

"I'll check out the bedroom." I motioned for Paige and Aunt Shirley to follow. I fished out my cell phone from my pocket, just in case I needed to snap pictures real quick and look for clues.

I pushed open the bedroom door and was immediately flooded with the smell of musty old man. Not a pleasant odor. Manning's bed was unmade and his clothes were strewn all over the floor. A couple boxes were pushed up against the wall, but he was nowhere to be seen.

"Where the heck is he?" Paige asked.

A scream reverberated throughout the small apartment, and the three of us took off for the sound.

We found Mrs. McElroy standing in the narrow hallway pointing wordlessly into the bathroom. It obviously wasn't going to be good news.

And just my luck it would be in the bathroom.

I looked up and caught Lovey's eye at the end of the hallway by the living room. I could tell we were thinking the same thing.

"Let me through. Let me through," Mr. McElroy demanded as he pushed his way past the people in the living room and shuffled toward his wife. "What's wrong, my pet?"

Mrs. McElroy still couldn't talk, only point. I gently pushed past Mrs. McElroy and braced myself for what I'd see.

And nothing could have prepared me for what I saw. Manning, face down on the linoleum floor, in a pile of his own vomit.

Aunt Shirley popped up behind me. "You think this is a good time to get a selfie with Manning's body? Be a cool way to introduce my new hairstyle to our *Gazette* readers."

CHAPTER 12

"Mr. Shifley, you need to call downstairs and let them know," Virginia whispered. She looked pale and scared.

Shifty didn't say a word. Instead, he kept his gaze glued to Manning.

"I can't believe he was really that sick," Lovey said. "I mean, to just up and die of the flu seems excessive."

I thought so too, which is why I wasn't sure it was strictly the flu. But before I said anything to anyone else, I wanted to check out a few things. I especially didn't like the way Shifley was staring at Manning.

"I'm gonna take a look at his room real quick," I said.

Neighbor 370 stuck out her cane and hit me in the shin. "Wait just a second there, young lady. I don't think you should be touching anything."

"I won't touch anything."

"What gives you the right to go back there to his bedroom?" Neighbor 370 challenged.

Aunt Shirley let out a cackle. "How about the fact she gives the chief of police a good time in—"

"Aunt Shirley!" I hissed. I could feel my face burn. While a part of me wanted to tape Aunt Shirley's vulgar mouth closed, the other part of me wanted to stick my tongue out at Neighbor 370 and say, "Yeah, so take that!" I didn't, of course. But I did make a point of knocking her cane away as I headed down the rest of the hall toward Manning's bedroom. I didn't have to look to know Aunt Shirley and Paige were following me.

"You're gonna check out those boxes, aren't you?" Aunt Shirley asked.

"Yep. I'm pretty sure the stolen merchandise from the pantry is in there."

Paige sighed. "So you're thinking this is more than an older man dying because he's been sick?"

I looked at Aunt Shirley before answering. "Yes, I do. I think there might be more to the story than he just up and died from the flu. Especially if we find stolen goods in here."

Aunt Shirley nodded her head. "Agreed."

"Do you want me to snap pictures while you call Garrett?" Paige asked. "This way you can deny all allegations."

"Good thinking." I'd been dating Garrett long enough to know if it turned out I was right, he wasn't going to be happy about this discovery. If he knew I was in the bedroom snooping around, he was going to be extra mad I got personally involved. I know it's probably blurring the lines a little, having Paige snap the pictures instead of me, but I still felt okay about it.

"Aunt Shirley, go grab a towel from the kitchen so we don't get fingerprints on the boxes."

"Got one right here." Lovey, Dotty, and Virginia were huddled together in the doorframe. Lovey held out a white dishcloth to Paige.

"You might want to hurry," Dotty said. "Mr. Shifley finally got his head out of his butt and he's called downstairs for help."

We all moved in closer as Paige wrapped the towel around her hand and carefully grabbed the middle of one of the cardboard boxes and lifted up the panel. We all leaned in to get a closer look inside. There were toiletries, medications, numerous packages of starter seeds for a vegetable garden and flower garden, utensils, and napkins. Nothing stood out to me as to why Manning would have stolen this particular shipment from the pantry.

"I'm going to assume these are the stolen boxes from the pantry," I said.

"Why would he steal them?" Lovey asked.

I shrugged and looked at Aunt Shirley. "I think it's time to call Garrett. I think Manning may have died from more than just sickness."

Virginia let out a gasp. "Do you really think so?"

I didn't say anything more. I took out my phone and dialed Garrett. The butterflies in the pit of my stomach were beginning to spread their wings. I suddenly had the urge to throw up.

He picked up on the second ring. "Hey, Sin. Not to worry, I'm working on the Aunt Shirley thing right now."

I cleared my throat. "Well, I'm calling for a different reason. You know how I came to the Manor to get some of Aunt Shirley's stuff?" I didn't wait for a reply. "Well, it seems Aunt Shirley's neighbor, Mr. Manning, is dead. He died in his bathroom. I thought you should know."

Silence. "Is this a police matter? I mean, I don't want to sound harsh, but don't people die there all the time?"

"Well, yes. And he *had* been sick. But…"

"But what?"

"He has some stolen items in his room."

"What?"

There was no way I could explain this rationally. "I just really think you should come over. I don't think it was natural causes."

Garrett sighed. "I'll be right there. Tell me you didn't touch anything."

I looked at Paige. "I didn't touch anything. Promise."

Garrett grunted and hung up.

"He's on his way," I told everyone.

I was about to have Paige lift the lid of another box when I heard Thomas Shifley yelling from the hallway. "Get away from there! You can't be in here."

"Give us one good reason why not?" Aunt Shirley shot back.

Shifley was saved from answering when a couple orderlies from downstairs arrived to help take out the body. I recognized one of them as Carl Baker from the other day. He stopped in his tracks and gave Shifley a hard stare.

Shifley herded us back out to the living room. It didn't take long before Sheri Daniels arrived looking angry and put out. I hoped Garrett hurried and got here before they started moving the body too much.

"What's going on here?" Sheri demanded.

"Manning is dead," Aunt Shirley said. "And he has a ton of stolen merchandise in his bedroom."

Sheri's eyes cut to Shifley before she ran down the hallway. She was back within seconds, her face pinched and red. "Where's the rest of it? Did anyone touch this stuff?"

Neighbor 370 pointed her cane at me.

Jeez, her and Manning must have gotten along swimmingly with all the cane pointing.

"I told her not to go in there," Neighbor 370 said.

"Am I interrupting?" Garrett asked as he and my brother, Matt, moved farther inside the apartment.

Sheri puffed out her chest. "I'm the Coordinator, Sheri Daniels."

"I'm Chief Kimble, and I received word there was a dead body."

"This is Oak Grove Manor business. Death of a resident does not require your help, Chief."

I bit back a chuckle and waited for Garrett to unleash on her. I wasn't disappointed.

"I've been informed that the deceased was found with stolen goods in his possession. I have probable cause. So if you will excuse me, I will be taking over from here."

His icy tone left no doubt that he didn't give two poops whether or not Sheri liked it. He was taking over.

"Our Executive Director, Lucy Stevenson, will be hearing about this," Sheri said.

"I can't wait," Garrett said dryly. "Until then, I expect all of you to wait here while we conduct our investigation."

For the first time Garrett took in Aunt Shirley's new look. "What did you do to your hair?"

Aunt Shirley smiled and patted her head. "You like?"

Garrett didn't say a word.

Matt walked over to where we were gathered. He, too, did a double-take at Aunt Shirley. "Nice hair, Aunt Shirley." I couldn't tell if he was lying. Sometimes cops have to be good at being deceitful.

Garrett sighed. "I'm going to take a look around the bedroom. No one leaves." He made a point to look at me before striding down the hall to Manning's bedroom.

"I hope this won't take too long," Mrs. McElroy said. "Our grandchildren are coming over for a visit in a couple hours. I don't want to miss them."

Paige, the comforter of the group, patted Mrs. McElroy on the arm. "I'm sure we'll be done by then."

"I need to sit down," Neighbor 370 complained. "My bunions are killing me."

I figured now was a good time to find out her name. I didn't want to have to call her Neighbor 370 forever. "I didn't catch your name."

Neighbor 370 scowled at me. "I didn't give it."

"Her name's Mildred Prittle," Aunt Shirley said. "And she's as big a pain in the butt as Manning was."

Before I could comment, a couple EMTs and our coroner, Melvin Collins, came rushing in from the hallway.

"Back there," Matt pointed.

I wasn't sure how they were all going to fit inside Manning's tiny bathroom.

Garrett squeezed by the group in the hallway and made his way toward us. He kept his eyes on me the whole time.

"I'm assuming the items in the box did not belong to Mr. Manning?" Garrett asked me.

"Why are you asking her?" Sheri demanded. "I'm the Coordinator in charge of this facility, and I'm pretty sure her and her dim-witted aunt are behind the thefts somehow."

Garrett's face went blank and his eyes hardened. "You are aware that this 'thief' and her 'dim-witted' aunt," his mouth quirked like he wanted to smile, "are practically my family, right? So keep it up, and we'll be having this talk downtown at the station."

I did a little dance inside. I wish my job allowed me to put people in their place. Instead it usually got me tangled up in murder.

Sheri's face turned red and her cheeks puffed in and out. "I became aware that an order I placed last week had recently gone missing from the pantry. I've been doing my best to find the culprits and have them arrested."

Garrett frowned. "Why the zealousness for a few stolen items? There didn't look to be too much in the boxes worth pressing charges over."

Sheri broke eye contact and refused to answer.

"Ms. Daniels, I've asked you a question."

Sheri sighed. "Because one item in particular isn't in the boxes. I already checked."

I could tell Garrett didn't like that answer. "What kind of item?"

"Let's just say it could be deadly in the wrong hands."

We all gasped.

Sheri Daniels sighed. "I placed an order through the greenhouse for castor beans to start new seedlings for the spring."

"And these castor beans are deadly?" Garrett asked.

Sheri Daniels pressed her lips together. "Yes. They contain ricin. If you grind the seeds up, it's an extremely dangerous poison."

Cha-ching...and a story is born!

CHAPTER 13

Chaos erupted in the tiny living room.

"Poison!" Lovey exclaimed. "Like we could all die?"

"How would we know if we were poisoned?" Dotty demanded.

"I don't feel too well," Mrs. McElroy said and swayed on her feet. Mr. McElroy caught her and lowered her to the couch.

"We need help!" Mr. McElroy exclaimed. "My wife has been poisoned!"

Garrett threw up his hands. "Calm down. Everyone take a deep breath and calm down. No one has been poisoned."

"How do you know?" Mildred said and slammed the end of her cane down on the floor repeatedly. "I myself feel kind of woozy."

I almost laughed out loud.

"Enough!" Garrett's voice rang out with enough command that pretty much everyone stopped what they were doing—even the emergency personnel people.

I looked nervously at Aunt Shirley. I didn't like when Garrett got all serious cop on me. It scared me. Always brought me around to how grave his job really was.

"You guys carry on," Garrett said to the EMTs, then turned to us. "You people stop the theatrics."

Mildred huffed but didn't say anything more.

I turned to Sheri. "Do you think Manning was the thief? The person that's been stealing from people's bedrooms and who stole from the pantry?"

Sheri shrugged. "Probably."

"So now Manning's the thief?" Aunt Shirley snorted. "A few minutes ago Ryli and I were the thieves. Maybe you stole the shipment and put it here after you killed Manning."

Sheri Daniels's mouth hung open. "I most certainly did not!"

"Or maybe Shifty here did it," Aunt Shirley continued. "He and Manning had a plan to steal the items, but Manning got greedy or something so Shifty here knocked him off."

"I did not!" Shifley exclaimed. "But I wouldn't put it past Manning to be the thief. I thought he'd been acting strange lately."

Since when?

Garrett closed his eyes and shook his head. "Just stop with the speculation. I only work with facts and motive. And I'll be the one to decide what those are."

I was about to say something about Thomas Shifley's perception of Manning's recent behavior when I caught Aunt Shirley's eye. She gave me a tiny shake of her head.

Great, I'm about to get in deep.

"So you don't think we need to worry?" Mr. McElroy said. "How're you feeling my love?"

Mrs. McElroy smiled. "I feel okay. I think the scare just made my heart race a little too fast."

"I know why Ryli, Paige, and Aunt Shirley are here," Garrett said. "Why are the rest of you here?"

"We heard shouting in the hallway," Lovey said. "So that's why me, Dotty, and Virginia are here."

"Same with us," Mr. McElroy said. "We heard the shouting in the hallway and checked it out."

"And you?" Garrett asked.

Mildred scowled. "Like Ray Manning, God rest his soul, I've never liked Shirley. I was glad when I heard she was leaving and wanted to make sure I got to see her off. Plus I heard the commotion in the hallway. I figured Shirley was behind it somehow."

I grabbed hold of Aunt Shirley before she could take a swing at Mildred.

"And who are you?" Garrett asked.

Shifley swallowed, his Adam's apple bobbing up and down. "My name is Thomas Shifley. I'm the orderly in charge of this floor."

"I call him Shifty," Aunt Shirley said. "Because that's exactly what he is."

Shifley's face turned red, and he looked like he wanted to strangle Aunt Shirley.

Garrett held up his hand. "I want everyone to go back to their apartments on this floor, and I'll be around shortly to ask questions. Aunt Shirley, Paige, and Ryli, you go back to Aunt Shirley's apartment. I want to speak to Ms. Daniels and Mr. Shifley alone."

"But I don't know anything!" Shifley whined. "I didn't do anything."

Garrett rubbed his temple. "This is going to be a long day. I can already tell."

I knew that look and what it meant. I didn't want to be around to see the fallout. I grabbed hold of Aunt Shirley and Paige and started for the door. Paige blew Matt a kiss as we left.

The McElroys and Mildred went straight into their apartments without saying a word. The rest of us stood out in the hallway, unsure as to what to do.

Lovey pointed to Aunt Shirley's hair. "I didn't think it was the appropriate time in Manning's apartment to tell you this, but I like your hair."

Virginia and Dotty nodded in agreement.

Should I be concerned they're all such good liars?

"Well, I think we deserve a drink," Dotty said. "Death will do that to you—even if you don't like the person that died. We'll talk with you guys later."

Virginia, Lovey, and Dottie went into Virginia's apartment while we went into Aunt Shirley's.

"Does this mean I don't get to leave this place?" Aunt Shirley grumbled.

For the first time in nearly an hour I felt light-hearted. I was hoping that's *exactly* what it meant. My good mood was momentarily put on hold when Hank's ringtone filled the air. I reached into my pocket, pulled out my cell phone, and put it on speaker. "Hey, Hank. I got you on speaker. What's up?"

"What's up?" he barked. I could imagine him yanking his unlit cigar out of his mouth. "How about the fact I just heard on the scanner there's been police and medics called out to Oak Grove Manor. How's that for what's up? What's going on over there?"

"Aunt Shirley's neighbor, Ray Manning, was found dead," I said.

"Was he involved in the theft story you were talking about earlier?"

"Looks that way."

"Who found him? And for your job's sake you better say you did!"

I rolled my eyes. "As a matter of fact, I did find him."

"Ha! That's my girl! Now get back here and write me a story."

"I have to wait for Garrett to come release us, then I'll be there."

"Make it fast, Sinclair. I want that story by press time!"

I smiled slyly into the phone. "So now I get two front-page stories, right?"

Hank didn't say anything.

"Right, Hank?"

"Fine. You can have front-page top half *and* bottom half if you get me that story!"

I hung up and let out a little victory shout. "Can you imagine? I'll have two front-page stories next week! Of course, I can't exactly call it a murder since we don't really know anything yet, but I can at least allude to stolen items and speculate on when the toxicology report comes back will it come back clean. Hopefully by the following week everything will be solved, and I can have *another* front-page story."

Paige clapped her hands together. "That's wonderful. I'm very proud of you."

"Yeah, yeah. Just great, Barbara Walters." Aunt Shirley thrust a pad of paper and pen in my hand. "Now, let's get down to brass tactics…suspects and motive."

"Why?" I asked. "Surely Garrett will have this wrapped up in a matter of hours."

"I wouldn't be too sure about that. You know how Ace can get sometimes."

I narrowed my eyes at her. Aunt Shirley knew how I felt about her little nickname for Garrett.

"Let's at least sit down and think this through," Paige said diplomatically.

I let her lead me to the sofa and sat down next to her. Aunt Shirley sat in her recliner and reached into the drawer of her end table. "Darn, I already packed away my new e-cig."

"Good," I said. "I hate when you smoke that thing."

Aunt Shirley scowled at me. "It helps me think. Sherlock Holmes had his pipe, and I have my e-cig."

I had to physically bite my lip to keep from retorting.

"We have Sheri Daniels and Shifty for sure." Aunt Shirley stopped talking and glared at me. "Start writing. You're the professional here."

Paige put her hand on my knee and gave me a gentle smile. Her way of saying we didn't need two murders this morning.

I put down Sheri Daniels and Thomas Shifley on the paper. I could only think of one other person who might know about the order that was stolen or who could have moved the order. "Kaylee?"

"Yes," Aunt Shirley agreed. "I don't think she did it, but she did have access."

I rested the pen against my chin. "I overheard Kaylee and Manning talking in the hall the other day, and Manning said a lot of people knew she put the boxes in the pantry. So there are more suspects here than we know."

"But the big question is why," Paige said. "Why kill Manning?"

Aunt Shirley leaned back in her recliner. "I've been thinking about how quick Shifty was to place blame on Manning being the thief and saying Manning was acting weird the last few days. What if the other recent thefts *were* in fact committed by Manning, or Manning somehow found out who was committing them and someone killed him to keep quiet?" Aunt Shirley frowned and shook her head. "I haven't quite figured out how the ricin plays a part as far as who knew castor beans were being shipped to the Manor and that they could be potentially poisonous. I sure didn't know. And the truth is, the whole ricin thing just may be a coincidence."

"You don't like coincidences," I reminded her.

"I know. Ace will send off for a tox report, which should come back fairly quickly because they'll rush it if they suspect foul play. Your job, Ryli, is to somehow sweet talk your man into sharing that information with you."

I let out a short laugh. "Garrett isn't going to tell me anything. I might be able to eavesdrop a little, but believe me, Garrett will not volunteer anything. The man is a vault when it comes to keeping secrets."

Aunt Shirley crossed her arms and snickered. "Well, you better learn how to crack that safe fast because we're gonna need to know if we're on the right track."

A few minutes later Garrett and Matt walked through the apartment door. I scooted over on the couch so Matt could sit next to Paige. "How'd it go?" I asked.

"Should have the toxicology report soon since we may know what we're looking for," Garrett said. "Talked with the two I kept, then talked with Virginia, Dotty, and Lovey. Officer Ryan took Mr. and Mrs. McElroy and Mildred Prittle."

"Who're you arresting for the murder?" Aunt Shirley demanded. "I'm sure it's that Sheri Daniels. She's also the ring leader for the thefts that are going on."

"First off, I'm not even sure there's a murder," Garrett said. "And second, *if* there's a burglary ring going on, it's for me to figure out, not you. And believe me, I'll be figuring it out soon."

"*If!*" Aunt Shirley cried. "Old Man Jenkins has had his bottle of Viagra stolen. How much more evidence do you need!"

Garrett blanched. "A lot more evidence."

Matt chuckled at Garrett's face.

"There's also more news," Garrett said hesitantly.

I narrowed my eyes at Garrett. "What's going on?"

He sighed. "There's good news and not-so-good news. I talked with the Executive Director, Lucy Stevenson. She's absolutely horrified that all this—possible murder and a possible burglary ring—could be going on under her nose. She's put out about the fact that not only didn't she know about the missing boxes from the pantry, but the fact other items have recently gone missing from residents' rooms. This has made it to where I could negotiate Aunt Shirley's return. Lucy said when I solve the case, Aunt Shirley can come back to stay."

I sucked in my breath. "But until it's solved?"

"She lives with you," Garrett said.

"Whoohoo!" Aunt Shirley exclaimed.

I closed my eyes at the dreaded words. If ever there was a time to interfere with an investigation, it was now. Somehow I'd find a way to hear the results of the toxicology test, and I'd do whatever I could to help solve this case fast.

We quickly gathered up some boxes and Garrett and Matt walked us down to the lobby to say goodbye. I turned to leave when Garrett grabbed my hand. "Hey, what do you know about this Virginia lady? She's the one you interviewed, right?"

I cocked my brow. "Why?"

Garrett sighed. "Just answer the question, please."

"Yes, she's the one I interviewed. I know her, Lovey, and Dotty have been friends for over sixty years. I know three of her husbands have died—but don't worry, they are easily explained deaths."

"How so?"

I told him how each husband had died. "I also know she's a really nice lady who likes to hang out with her friends and drink cocktails. Harmless, really."

"Did she mention threatening letters?"

I nodded my head. "Oh, yeah. She said that Manning would send her threatening letters all the time. Like mean, nasty letters."

"Does she still have them?"

"No. I think they burned them in a silly ritual and then had more drinks." I said it like it was a joke, but I could tell he wasn't buying it. "What's going on?"

No surprise he ignored my question. "Did Virginia ever mention writing threatening notes to Manning?"

I shook my head. "If you've found something that points to Virginia leaving threatening notes to Manning, believe me, it was done in self-defense. Virginia did not do this! She is the victim here. Manning was a nasty man. I had my own run-ins with him numerous times."

I suddenly wondered if I should mention overhearing Kaylee threaten to kill Manning. I didn't want to throw Kaylee under the bus, but I also didn't want Garrett focusing too much on Virginia and not looking at other suspects.

"I do know of something I haven't told you yet. I *may* have overheard Kaylee Jones threaten to kill Manning the other day."

"What? Who's Kaylee Jones?" He held up his hand. "No, never mind. I'll start from the bottom and work my way up the suspect list. Thanks for the information."

He leaned over and gave me a kiss. It almost made me feel better for throwing Kaylee under the bus.

CHAPTER 14

Paige decided to go home to get supper ready for Matt, and since I wasn't expecting Garrett to finish up anytime soon, Aunt Shirley and I headed over to see Mom. Even though I love spending time with my mom, this time I went to sulk over having to be Aunt Shirley's caregiver. After mom stopped hyperventilating over Aunt Shirley's new hairdo, we brought her up to speed over finding Manning's dead body. By the time we finished our story, the dinner she was making for her and Doc was finished.

"You want to stay for dinner, dear?" Mom asked.

I sighed. Even though I was tempted to say yes, I declined. I didn't figure she wanted two extra wheels at her romantic dinner. And if anyone deserved happiness, it was my mom.

"Better not. I think Garrett might stop over to grab a quick bite before heading back to the office." I had no idea if it was true or not, but it sounded plausible.

"Don't forget we're voting on a new pastor tomorrow after church." Since we'd been months without a full-time preacher, we were really hoping this guy was going to work out. "Please try to keep Aunt Shirley in line."

I looked over at Aunt Shirley zipping up her camo parka. The purple in her shaved head glared back at me. "No promises."

I shoved Aunt Shirley into the Falcon and headed back to my place. I definitely deserved a *huge* glass of wine with dinner…or the whole dang bottle!

"What's for dinner?" Aunt Shirley asked. "I'm starving. Finding a dead body always takes it out of me."

"I'm sure," I said dryly.

My phone beeped and I read the text message. It was from Garrett. He was going to stop by and grab a bite to eat with us before heading back to the station to relieve Officer Ryan. While I was happy he was coming over, I had to wonder if he had an ulterior motive.

Fifteen minutes later Garrett parked his police-issued vehicle in the driveway and was greeted promptly by Miss Molly. He gave her a few scratches before she turned her nose up and walked away.

"Will I have better luck with you?" he teased.

I wrapped my arms around his neck and let him know he would indeed.

"I only have about half an hour before I need to get back," Garrett grinned. "Save that for later."

I blushed and sashayed into the kitchen to heat up tomato soup and start preparations for grilled cheese sandwiches. Garrett shredded cheese to put in the tomato soup.

Aunt Shirley was busy in my room unpacking her suitcase and makeup travel case. The fact her makeup bag was larger than her suitcase was no surprise. She firmly believed you weren't put together unless you had your makeup on—especially your lipstick.

"Please tell me you'll have this solved quickly," I pleaded. "I don't know how many days I can live with her."

Garrett put down the grater and wrapped his arms around me. He brushed a curl off my cheek. "I promise to have this wrapped up quickly."

104

He ran his thumb over my bottom lip and I shivered. I leaned up on my tiptoes and kissed him fully on the mouth.

"Get a room you two," Aunt Shirley said as she walked into the open kitchen.

I groaned and grabbed hold of Garrett's shirt, not wanting to let him go. "We can't get a room," I said. "You're in it."

Garrett chuckled and rested his lips on my forehead.

"Don't burn my sandwich." Aunt Shirley leaned against the counter bar that separated my kitchen and living room. "And I'm cold. I'd like some hot tea."

"I'll get it," Garrett said. He put the platter of shredded cheese on the table and grabbed a coffee cup out of the cupboard. He filled it with water and popped it in the microwave to heat.

"Ya know," Aunt Shirley said to Garrett, "you ain't getting any younger, Ace. You want kids someday?"

Garrett reeled back like he'd been slapped. "Excuse me?"

I was proud of him for ignoring the Ace remark.

"I said you wanting kids someday? It's an easy question."

"Maybe," Garrett hedged, stealing a look at me.

"Well," Aunt Shirley continued, "I ain't no doctor, but I think it's safe to say you shouldn't be standing so close to the microwave. I read on the Internet they have these little radioactive waves or something like that that kills off swimmers. And seeing as how you're so old, you might need to save all the swimmers you can so you can at least father one kid."

Garrett's face went from red to pink to red again. I tried not to laugh, but I couldn't help it.

He turned and glared at me. "It's not funny. And I'll have you know," he went on, pointing his finger at Aunt Shirley, "that my *swimmers* are just fine, thank you."

I couldn't help it, I laughed so hard I snorted. I'd been so stressed the whole day that it felt great to just let loose. Tears were falling from my eyes. "I so needed that."

Garrett's mouth twitched as he tried not to smile. "Glad me and my swimmers could help."

I flipped the last sandwich as Garrett finished setting the table. As we all sat down to eat, I begrudgingly had to admit it actually felt nice having Aunt Shirley there. Of course, she was stuffing her mouth with grilled cheese so she couldn't talk, which I'm sure helped a lot.

"By the way," Garrett said nonchalantly. "Nearly every person I spoke with has Ray Manning and Aunt Shirley fighting in the halls on a couple different occasions this week. Some reported hearing her threaten to kill him. Maybe even kill him five different ways."

Aunt Shirley laughed loudly at Garrett's revelation. "You don't really think I poisoned that guy, do you?"

"No," Garrett said. "Just making conversation. And no one is saying he was poisoned."

Aunt Shirley cackled. "Please. Me use poison? Nope. If I were gonna kill that blowhard Manning, I'd have sewed his mouth shut so he couldn't yell at me as I beat him to death with his stupid cane."

"I didn't hear a word," Garrett said and continued eating his grilled cheese sandwich.

I'd just finished putting the final touches on my Manning submission to Hank when Aunt Shirley walked into the room the next morning. She was wearing black pants with a red sweater. That was all perfectly fine, if you ignored the clash of shocking purple hair.

What wasn't perfectly fine was the fact the red sweater had a huge heart on it, and the inside of the heart was filled with about one hundred tiny rhinestones. When she walked into the room, the light reflected off her rhinestones and I went blind.

Aunt Shirley did a twirl. "You like? It's my dressy Valentine's Day sweater I ordered for myself. I knew Old Man Jenkins would love it."

"You can't wear that to church," I said and rubbed my eyes. "You can't wear that anywhere for that matter."

"And why not?"

"Why not? Because it just blinded me. You look like a freaking disco ball! When Pastor Tim gets up to preach you'll blind him, he'll fall off the platform, hit his head on the altar, get a concussion, and you will single-handedly be responsible for him not coming to our church. And then Mom will be so mad—at both of us."

Aunt Shirley snorted. "Won't happen. Now let's go before all the good seats are taken."

I sighed as we threw on our coats and hopped in the Falcon. We made it to church in less than five minutes. Unfortunately, the church was already packed by the time we made our way through the front door. This was sure to be one of the most important Sundays since Pastor Williams announced his resignation.

I personally liked Pastor Tim and his family. He was young, had two kids, and he let us use his first name when we addressed him.

The bad thing about being right on time for church means you have to sit in the first three rows of pews. The early birds get the back of the church. Luckily Mom and Paige had saved us spots in the middle. By the time we sat down the first song had already started.

I took off my coat at the end of the song and laid it over the back of the pew and sat down. Aunt Shirley did the same. Our church superintendent was in attendance for the counting of the votes after church. He made the introductions of Pastor Tim and his family before handing the pulpit over to Pastor Tim.

"I better take notes," Aunt Shirley whispered and reached next to her for her purse. Unfortunately, the sudden movement caused the rhinestones in her sweater to catch the lights. And catch Pastor Tim's eyes.

"Omigosh," I hissed. "Stop moving! I told you this would happen."

Pastor Tim shook his head as if to clear it and started his sermon again.

"Found it." Aunt Shirley swung back around and caused Pastor Tim to be blinded once again.

"Stop moving!" I whispered louder. "You're blinding the pastor!"

"Who is?" Aunt Shirley demanded and twisted around in her seat to look over her right shoulder and then twisted again to look over her left shoulder. Each rotation hit Pastor Tim in the face— along with the choir sitting behind him, and a few unfortunate front-row members who'd turned around in their pews to see what was going on.

Cries of pain rang out throughout the church.

"Throw a coat over her," Mom hissed. "She's going to blind the whole church!"

I grabbed my coat off the back of the pew, threw it around Aunt Shirley, and tied the sleeves behind her neck.

The little Blackstone boy, who was about five, turned around in his pew and smiled shyly at Aunt Shirley. His two front teeth were missing. "You thparkle like an angel," he whispered. There was no denying the awe in his voice.

"Thank you," Aunt Shirley whispered back. She put her fingers to her lips. "But shhh, I'm supposed to be in disguise."

I didn't know whether to laugh or cry at her response.

The rest of the service went off without a hitch. Pastor Tim was able to get back on track and finish his sermon, and I hoped like heck the little debacle didn't keep him from leading our church. I was half afraid he'd back out if he thought he had to deal with Aunt Shirley every Sunday.

After the vote, the congregation filed out of the church and into the parking lot. I zipped my coat and wrapped my scarf securely around my neck. The wind had picked up and I was getting cold.

I was talking with Mom and Paige when Garrett pulled up next to the Falcon. Aunt Shirley excused herself from the group of older ladies she was talking with to come over and join us.

Garrett rolled down his window. "Hey, I know I was supposed to try and stop by for Sunday lunch, but I'm going to head on over to the Manor and talk with both Lucy Stevenson and Sheri Daniels."

"Why?" I asked. "Did you find out something?"

Garrett leveled his gaze at me and frowned. "You know I'm not telling you anything."

I shrugged and gave him my best innocent smile. "You know I was only teasing."

Not.

"Sorry you can't make it, Garrett," Mom said then turned to me. "But you two are coming over, right?"

I was about to nod my head when Aunt Shirley grabbed her stomach, bent over, and started moaning. "I don't think I can right now. I seem to be having some stomach issues."

"Oh great," I mumbled. "Can't she go home with you, Mom?"

"No!" Aunt Shirley cried. "I need to go to your house. I feel comfortable there."

I rolled my eyes at Garrett and he laughed. "Well, I think that's my cue to leave. Do you want me to stop by after work or do you want to come out to the house?"

Sunday nights I usually spent at Garrett's house. We'd pop popcorn and catch up on our DVR'd shows for the week. "I'll come on out around six."

Garrett said goodbye and pointed his truck in the direction of the Manor.

"Well Paige," Mom said, "it looks like it's just you, me, and Martin for lunch."

"Actually," Aunt Shirley said, "I need Paige. I have something sexy for her for Valentine's Day. Might help with giving me a baby to bounce on my knee soon."

Paige's face turned red. "I don't even want to know."

Aunt Shirley turned to Mom. "Sorry, Janine, we'll need to take a rain check."

Mom frowned. "Okay. Guess it's just me and Martin for lunch."

We waved goodbye to Mom with a promise to call later to let her know how Aunt Shirley was feeling. I felt guilty for lying. One look at Aunt Shirley and I knew she was perfectly fine.

"This is what we're gonna do," Aunt Shirley said once I pulled out of the church parking lot. "While Garrett is talking with Lucy and Sheri, we're going to be looking through Sheri's house for stolen goods."

"Uh, no we're not," I said. "I'm not breaking into anyone's house."

"Don't be a sissy," Aunt Shirley snorted. "I used to do this stuff all the time when I was a private investigator. And the best part about doing this during winter...we all have gloves with us, so we won't leave fingerprints."

"What makes you think she's keeping stolen goods at her house?" I asked.

Aunt Shirley rolled her eyes. "You amateur. Do you really think she's going to leave that kind of evidence hanging around the Manor? And at this point everyone is a suspect until we eliminate them. And I think right now until we can prove otherwise, we have to believe that the person with the stolen goods is also the killer that murdered Manning."

"We're not even sure Manning *was* murdered," I said.

"It was murder," Aunt Shirley said. "It's always murder."

I rolled my eyes. "It's *not* always murder. People *can* die from natural causes, you know?"

"Why did I have to come along?" Paige asked from the backseat.

"Misery loves company," I said.

CHAPTER 15

"I still can't believe you were able to get Sheri's address so quickly," Paige said.

Aunt Shirley turned and smirked at Paige. "Old Man Jenkins retired from the post office, and she was on his route. He said she used to get packages that were unmarked and looked like those naughty packages you can get in the mail. But I'm thinking now maybe it was like a poison-of-the-month club she was involved in."

I laughed. "That's quite a far-reaching speculation."

Aunt Shirley grinned. "Yeah, even for me."

"And he just offered to tell you where she lived?" Paige asked.

"When I told him I couldn't come back to the Manor until I proved Sheri was the murderer, he gave me her address."

I shook my head at Aunt Shirley's response. "Wait. So now suddenly you want to go back to the Manor?"

Aunt Shirley shrugged. "I don't know. I kinda feel like you're smothering me a little. I miss having my own space."

My mouth dropped open. "*I'm* smothering *you*? Are you serious?"

"Don't go gettin' all offended. Jeez. You can be so sensitive sometimes."

I could feel my eyes cross. I was afraid I'd word vomit a plethora of things I couldn't take back, so I focused on keeping my mouth shut.

Paige leaned forward from the backseat. "I thought we weren't sure Sheri was the murderer or even if there is a murder."

"I'm not convinced," I said. "Nor do I think for one minute she's stealing from residents."

"Like I said, this is the best way to eliminate suspects," countered Aunt Shirley. "Turn here. It shouldn't be but a couple miles up this road. Old Man Jenkins said it's a purple house with black shutters."

"What is she a witch?" I snorted.

I turned onto the gravel road. I admit I was nervous about breaking in. It wouldn't be my first time to break into a house with Aunt Shirley, but I wasn't sure what to expect out here. I'd think this far out in the country Sheri would have dogs for protection, which could mean we were all in big trouble.

Her house wasn't hard to miss. It actually was purple with black shutters. I turned into her short driveway and cut the engine. I listened for barking but didn't hear any.

"Paige, you keep a lookout for anything suspicious," Aunt Shirley directed and tossed her a referee's whistle she'd plucked out of her purse.

Paige caught the whistle and grinned. "Got it."

I said a quick prayer and exited the Falcon. I pulled on my gloves and walked with Aunt Shirley up to the front of the house. So far everything looked quiet.

"Let's look under the mat for a key before we use a credit card," Aunt Shirley said. The last time we broke into a house, we used the old credit card trick.

Luck was with us, and I pulled out a key from under the mat. I gently pushed open the front door and motioned for Aunt Shirley to follow.

Sheri's house was pretty much a standard ranch-style layout. The front door opened into the living room. We walked through it and into the dining room. An archway to the right led to the kitchen, while an archway to the left led to a darkened hallway.

Aunt Shirley and I quietly made our way down the narrow hallway. I opened the first door on the right and walked into Sheri's office.

Aunt Shirley grunted. "You seem to be on a roll today. First you find a key so you don't have to break in, and now you found the office on the first try. I say we buy a lottery ticket after this."

I smiled. "I'll take this half. You take that half." I walked over to a file cabinet and tugged it open. Not even locked. Obviously Sheri wasn't concerned about anyone getting into her files.

The first file contained everyday receipts she was obviously storing up for tax season. I quickly leafed through the files but didn't see anything suspicious. Nothing labeled 'Money From Stolen Goods' or anything like that.

"Nothing here," Aunt Shirley said. "I say we find her bedroom and go through her stuff."

I stared at her. "I'm pretty sure she's not keeping extra dentures or wallets or Viagra pills in her bedroom. I'm not looking through her stuff."

Aunt Shirley huffed. "If we don't turn over every stone, we can't really eliminate her."

I sighed. "Fine. But let's make it quick before we get caught."

I closed the office door behind me and headed toward the other door down the hall. We'd only made it a few steps before we heard Paige's whistle going off with so much fierceness you'd have thought a tornado was coming.

"Let's go!" I grabbed Aunt Shirley's parka and started dragging her down the hallway toward the front door.

"We can't go yet. We haven't checked her room or anything."

I threw my hands up in the air. "Are you insane? I know you hear Paige yelling and blowing the whistle. Obviously something is wrong!"

"Paige has a tendency to overreact. I bet it's just a swarm of bees or something."

I pursed my lips at her. "Get out now or I leave you here."

Aunt Shirley huffed and pushed me forward. "Fine. But for the record I'm totally against this."

"For the record, I couldn't care less."

We quickly walked back through the house exactly as we came, careful not to touch anything. I opened the front door and saw Paige hanging out the back window of the Falcon, blowing the whistle as hard as she could. I looked up the road but couldn't see anyone coming.

And then I heard it.

A deep, low growl.

I looked down into the ugliest, beadiest black eyes I'd ever seen. The tiny dog bared his teeth—which were almost as big as his whole body. That set off the other dogs to growl and bark.

"That's one ugly dog!" Aunt Shirley exclaimed as she took a step back into the house.

"We're surrounded!" Paige yelled from the car.

I realized she was right. Not counting the one currently showing off his wicked set of teeth, there must have been seven or eight more beasts yapping and running around like chickens with their heads cut off.

"Well, now we know why Sheri pretty much leaves everything open," Aunt Shirley said dryly.

"Who keeps a pack of wild Chihuahuas as attack dogs?" I asked.

Aunt Shirley peered around my shoulder and stared out at the army of death surrounding us. "Obviously that nut Sheri does."

I took a deep breath and tried to think of a plan. "Remember that scary movie you made me watch when I was a kid where the family had the demon-possessed dog? *Cujo* wasn't it? Now I know how that family felt. Only for us it's worse because there are like eight pissed off puppies ready to eat us alive!"

"I say we make a run for it and hope for the best," Aunt Shirley said. "And for the record, this definitely bumps Sheri up higher on my suspect list."

I silently agreed.

"Paige," I yelled over the barking dogs, "open the front passenger door when we get close so we can jump in!"

Paige stuck her thumb out the window in acknowledgment. She crawled into the front passenger seat and gave me a nod.

"On the count of three we run." I yanked the car keys out of my coat pocket. "One, two—"

"Wait!" Aunt Shirley cried and grabbed hold of my arm. "What about locking the door?"

"We aren't taking the time to lock the door," I said. "When I get to three you take off running and I'll stick the key back under the mat and be right behind you. Maybe she won't notice the front door is unlocked. Or if she does maybe she'll think she accidently left it that way."

Aunt Shirley nodded. "Okay. That seems reasonable. I mean, as reasonable as can be when death dogs are trying to tear you limb from limb."

"Ready? One, two, three!"

Aunt Shirley shot out from behind me and sprinted down the two steps before I could even blink. For an old lady she could move. I bent down and shoved the key under the mat, yanked the front door closed, shot up in the air, and took off down the stairs. It wasn't until I hit the bottom step that I noticed Aunt Shirley had fallen.

There were eight tiny Chihuahuas circling her prone body like vultures circling a carcass. Luckily she had that ridiculous camouflage parka she loves on and it cushioned her fall. Unfortunately the bulk made it so she couldn't get up quickly.

I reached up and took off my scarf, wrapped it once around my hand, and started swinging it around in the air. "Shoo! Get back!" I managed to get to Aunt Shirley's side unbitten.

"Help! It's biting me!" Aunt Shirley screamed.

"It's not biting you," I said as I lifted her up off the ground. "It's just pawing at you."

"I'm gonna need a rabies shot! You better run me straight to Doc Powell after this."

118

I rolled my eyes and dragged her along beside me. The dogs were keeping up with us, circling, snarling, snapping the whole way.

We were about five feet from the door when Aunt Shirley let out a blood-curdling scream. She yanked herself from my grasp and started spinning in circles, still screaming. Three of the dogs had latched onto the bottom of her parka and were holding on for dear life—with their teeth. The more she spun, the higher off the ground the dogs got...and the bigger their beady little eyes got. I wasn't sure who was more scared.

I couldn't help it. I started to laugh.

"It's not funny!" Aunt Shirley yelled. "These little demons better hope they don't tear my favorite coat."

I motioned for Paige—whose mouth was hanging open—to open the door. She pushed the door open, and three dogs ran to get into the Falcon. Paige screamed and slammed the door shut.

"Open the door!" Aunt Shirley hollered. "I'm gonna puke if I keep spinning."

Paige opened the car door once again, this time swinging her coat at the dogs that tried to jump in. Aunt Shirley and I bolted for the car and Paige scrambled into the backseat. I reached down and plucked off the three dogs hanging from Aunt Shirley's coat. When the dogs were gone, I shoved Aunt Shirley head first into the car, dove in beside her, and slammed the door shut.

"Gimme the keys." Aunt Shirley waved her right hand under my nose. "Since I'm in the driver's seat I'll drive."

I was breathing heavy but still managed a laugh. "Not on your life."

Aunt Shirley raised an eyebrow at me. "This used to be my car. I'm in the driver's seat, and I say I'm driving."

"You don't have a valid driver's license," I countered.

Our argument was interrupted by the yapping and clawing of tiny nails on the Falcon's door. No way was I letting the paint get scratched up by a bunch of angry Chihuahuas.

I thrust the keys into Aunt Shirley's hand. "Go, go! I don't want the paint scratched."

With a victory whoop Aunt Shirley grabbed the keys, stuck them in the ignition, put the Falcon in drive, and slammed down on the gas pedal. The Falcon took off like a rocket, causing me to tumble back and hit my head on the window.

"Slow down!" Paige cried. "You might hit one of the dogs."

Aunt Shirley snorted. "Those demons from hell will get out of the way, believe me."

I turned around in my seat and looked out the rear window. Aunt Shirley was right. All eight dogs were running around yapping. Some were jumping in the air snarling…but all of them had gotten out of the way. And something told me they would soon be plotting their revenge.

CHAPTER 16

"Thanks for letting us stay tonight." I grabbed the bowl of freshly popped popcorn off the kitchen counter while Garrett grabbed two bottled waters out of the refrigerator.

Garrett chuckled. "When I said yes, I thought it was just going to be you. I didn't realize we'd be babysitting Aunt Shirley."

"I don't need no stinking babysitter," Aunt Shirley yelled from the living room. "I can hear you. You realize that, right?"

Garrett grinned wickedly at me but spoke to Aunt Shirley. "Yep. That's why I said it loud enough for you to hear."

I gave him a light slap on the arm. "Play nice. I couldn't just leave her at my place alone overnight."

"Yes, you could. You realize she's a grown woman who has lived on her own for years."

After the run-in over at Sheri's house, I didn't want to take my chances of Sheri finding out and coming after us. I'm not sure how I convinced myself she might find out, but I did. And Aunt Shirley's constant whining about being left alone for the killer to get her didn't help. Of course, I couldn't explain that to Garrett unless I wanted to be thrown in jail for breaking and entering.

Instead of replying, I shifted the bowl to the side, stood on tiptoe, and leaned in and kissed him. The feel of his rough lips on mine gave me instant goosebumps.

"What's keeping you so long?" Aunt Shirley bellowed. "My beer wants some popcorn."

Garrett and I both growled. I wanted nothing more than to drop the popcorn and go straight upstairs. Instead, I was being summonsed to watch Aunt Shirley's favorite movie, *Dirty Harry.*

"Later," Garret whispered against my lips.

"I'll hold you to that."

Fortunately, later was much sooner than I thought. Aunt Shirley's downfall was stretching out on the couch with a pillow. She didn't even make it ten minutes into the movie before she started snoring. Garrett clicked off the TV, and I draped a blanket over her.

Garrett stood at the bottom of the curved staircase and motioned me over. He wrapped his arm around me and we walked up the stairs silently so we didn't wake Aunt Shirley.

"I need to get to the station," Garrett said as he walked out of his walk-in closet. "What's on your agenda today?"

I smiled at him. "Are you afraid I'm going to do something I'm not supposed to do?"

He chuckled. "I'm always afraid of that with you. I'll start coffee if you want to come down."

I grabbed some clothes out of the dresser, brushed my teeth, then made my way downstairs. I wanted to get Aunt Shirley and me to the newspaper office as early as possible to start researching backgrounds on my list of suspects for the recent thefts. So far I had Sheri Daniels, Thomas Shifley, and Kaylee Jones. I was also tossing around with putting Lucy Stevenson on the list of suspects. I really didn't think she was guilty, but my list of suspects was shockingly short.

Aunt Shirley and Garrett were already in the kitchen when I shuffled in for my morning cup of coffee. I was instantly on guard. Those two could barely stand being in the same room without tearing into each other.

"About time," Aunt Shirley grumbled. "I thought maybe he sexed you to death."

Garrett chuckled, and I choked on the drink I was about to take. "Jeez, do you have to be so crass?"

Garrett's cell phone lit up.

"Excuse me. I've been waiting for this call." He walked out of the kitchen to the far end of the living room. The fact he was standing with his back to me let me know he wanted to keep the conversation private.

I went to the coffee pot and poured a cup. I was pretty sure I knew what the phone call was about. "Do you suppose it's the toxicology report?"

No answer.

I turned to repeat the question, figuring Aunt Shirley had forgotten to put in her hearing aid—the one she claims to never wear—only to find I was looking at an empty chair. Fearing the worst, I set my coffee down on the kitchen table and hurried into the living room.

"What are you doing?" Garrett demanded.

Aunt Shirley popped up next to the end table where she had been kneeling. "I dropped my hearing aid last night."

Garrett narrowed his eyes at her. "I thought you didn't wear a hearing aid?"

Aunt Shirley shrugged.

"And I suppose you heard nothing of my private conversation?" Garrett asked.

"Didn't you hear me just say I forgot to put in my hearing aid? I didn't hear nothin' I tell you. Nothing!"

Methinks thou dost protest too much.

Garrett stared her down. Usually when he does that to me I fold like a house of cards.

Aunt Shirley laughed. "Stare all you want. Once when I was a private investigator I was kidnapped and tortured for the information I had."

I snorted. "And let me guess, Robert Redford was the one that kidnapped you?"

Aunt Shirley scowled. "No, Sherlock. It was a Mafia guy who tortured me. Pulled off one of my fingernails before I got the drop on him." She looked down at her pinky. "Darn thing never did grow back right."

I looked at Garrett. His eyebrows were nearly to his hairline. Sometimes it was hard to tell the truth from a lie with Aunt Shirley.

"I'm late," he said and leaned over to kiss my cheek. "I'll check in with you today to see how things are going. I have some leads to run, so I may be late tonight."

Aunt Shirley crossed her arms. "Don't worry. We have leads of our own to run today, too."

"No, you don't," Garrett said. "This is police business."

I didn't want the age-old argument to start up again. "She means we have leads on a story we're doing."

I didn't say anything to Aunt Shirley about eavesdropping until we got to the office. I was still wrestling with the guilt of her garnishing information from Garrett in a sneaky way.

"Morning you two," Mindy called out when we walked in. "I was just getting ready to make a cup of tea. Do you want some?" Her voice faded when she looked at Aunt Shirley for the first time.

"You like?" Aunt Shirley asked.

Mindy bobbed her head up and down so fast she could have been a bobble-head. "It's youthful. And the color is amazing."

Mindy was such a good woman…and a terrible liar.

I didn't want her to squirm anymore. "What kind are we drinking today?"

Mindy came out of her daze and smiled at me. "It's a grapefruit and strawberry blend. My new favorite."

Aunt Shirley made a face. "This is why we should be able to have tiny bottles of booze in our desk. Alone it sounds gross, but throw some rum in it and we have a party!"

I bit back a laugh. I didn't want to hurt Mindy's feelings, but Aunt Shirley was on to something. Some of Mindy's teas were pretty good. Others were so bad words couldn't do them justice.

"So where're we at with the Manning death?" Mindy set down two cups of tea. "Do we know if it was a murder or just an unfortunate death?"

"There's been no confirmation yet of our suspicions," I said.

Aunt Shirley made a wrong-answer buzzer noise. "Thanks for playing, but no dice. I happen to know he died from ricin poison."

"I *knew* you were eavesdropping this morning!" I exclaimed. "Forgot your hearing aid, my butt."

Aunt Shirley smiled. "Guilty. And it's a good thing I did eavesdrop, because lover boy wasn't going to tell you a thing."

"Ricin?" Mindy mused. "I'm not sure I'm familiar with that."

I turned on my computer and signed in. I pulled up Google and found information on ricin poisoning in castor beans. "Looks like ricin is a poison found in castor beans. If castor beans are chewed and swallowed, they release ricin poison. Death could occur anywhere from six hours to a few days."

"So Ray Manning ate the castor beans?" Mindy asked.

Aunt Shirley chuckled. "How did that idiot not know he was eating castor beans? And this just proves that Sheri Daniels is the murderer."

"How so?" I asked.

"She admitted to ordering the castor beans," Aunt Shirley said.

"But we didn't find anything at her house," I reminded Aunt Shirley.

"At her house?" Mindy asked. "What am I missing?"

I gave her a brief rundown on everything we knew so far, including yesterday's escapades at Sheri's house...ending with the yapping dogs. By the time I finished, Mindy was laughing and wiping tears from her eyes.

"I can't believe Chihuahuas were hanging from your coat," Mindy said. "I'm almost sorry I missed it."

Ever since I started *innocently* stumbling upon dead bodies, Hank has been more and more adamant Mindy and I don't spend as much time together. I'd be insulted if I didn't understand where he was coming from.

"So somehow Ray Manning ate castor bean seeds but didn't know it," Mindy mused. "How can that be? Wouldn't he know if he ate something that crunchy and nasty?"

I sucked in my breath and looked at Aunt Shirley. I could tell by the slow smile she knew what I was thinking. She nodded to me.

I let out a shaky laugh. "I think I know what he ate that killed him. Chocolate covered espresso beans."

Mindy scrunched her nose. "Yuck. I hate those things. Did you see him eat them recently?"

Aunt Shirley nodded her head. "Yes. A couple different times."

"I'm not sure this proves Sheri is the murderer," I argued. "Think about it. Thomas Shifley knew he ate them, Kaylee knew because she placed the order, and everyone on his floor knew."

Aunt Shirley narrowed her eyes at me. "What're you saying?"

I took a deep breath. "I think we need to add one more person to the list of suspects. I think we need to add Virginia Webber to the list."

"Why?" Aunt Shirley demanded. "Just because she's had three husbands die doesn't mean she killed Manning."

I rolled my eyes. "You've been suspicious of her since before we even met her."

"I know. But now that I know her, I've decided I like her. I don't think she killed Manning."

"Why?" I asked, throwing her question right back at her.

"Because she makes a killer drink," Aunt Shirley said smoothly. "No one that gifted at mixing can be a murderer."

Dear Lord, give me strength.

I sent Mindy an exasperated look. Leave it to Aunt Shirley to decide someone isn't guilty because they can mix an amazing alcoholic drink. "You know it doesn't work that way. We have to add her. Remember the first day we met Lovey and Dotty? They talked about how Manning had been harassing Virginia, and we heard them mention the notes he'd been leaving." I looked pointedly at Aunt Shirley. "And I happen to know they found a letter from Virginia in Manning's apartment. Garrett didn't say exactly what it said, but I'm assuming she threatened him. Maybe she took care of it herself."

Aunt Shirley crossed her arms. "Fine. We'll add her to the list, but I'm not happy about it."

"Duly noted," I said dryly. "I say we go to the Manor and talk with some of our suspects."

"I suggest," Hank said crossly as he walked up behind me, "that you go down to the police station and ask that boyfriend of yours for a quote on the death of this Ray Manning character."

"On it," I said.

Hank did a double-take at Aunt Shirley. "What in tarnation happened to your hair?"

Aunt Shirley made a face at Hank. "It's new and modern. It's all the rage and it's awesome."

Hank shoved his unlit cigar in his mouth. "Whatever you tell yourself, Tinker Bell."

I grabbed hold of Aunt Shirley before she could respond. "We're going. You'll have something in writing by the end of the day."

"Be careful," Mindy said. "It's starting to get serious."

Old-Fashioned Murder

CHAPTER 17

Aunt Shirley and I headed off toward the police station. I have to admit, I was curious what Garrett would tell me. I parked in the station parking lot and strolled inside. Claire Hickman was working dispatch.

"Good morning," Claire called out. "Oh, Shirley, I love your hair!"

I tried not to laugh. Of course Claire would. She had a fashion sense all her own.

"Thanks. I just got it done."

"What's new with you, Ryli?" Claire asked.

"Not much, Claire." I took off my gloves and shoved them in my coat pocket. "What about you? How are the fur babies?" Claire had two miniature poodles that went everywhere with her.

Claire beamed at me. "Minnie and Fifi are fabulous. Thanks for asking."

"Glad to hear it," I said. "And I love the coloring of today's outfit."

Claire smoothed down the crush of the dark purple velour suit she had on. Claire wore a different colored velour suit pretty much every day of the week. Her love affair with crushed velour was well known. "I love this one, too. Chief Kimble is in his office if you ladies want to go on back."

We thanked her and ambled down the hallway to Garrett's office. I knocked once and opened the door, but waited until he motioned us inside.

"Sin, nice to see you." He was using the nickname he gave me. That usually meant he knew I was up to no good. "And Aunt Shirley. To what do I owe the pleasure of this lovely visit?"

I resisted the urge to stick my tongue out at him. Instead, I walked around his desk and gave him a kiss on the cheek. I was pleased to see he'd put a couple pictures of me on his desk. Usually Garrett kept his office empty of any personal items.

Garrett smiled at me. "I'm sure you're here for more reasons than to just give me a kiss."

Aunt Shirley sat down in a chair across from his desk. "We're here to talk about Manning. The paper *and* the citizens of Granville want answers."

I rolled my eyes at Garrett. "We're actually here on official newspaper business. Hank wants to know about Ray Manning and if you are calling his death a homicide or was it a natural causes death?"

I knew I had to keep up the pretense of not knowing it was ricin that killed Manning, otherwise he'd know Aunt Shirley eavesdropped on his conversation that morning. He already suspected. I didn't want to give him proof.

I walked over and sat in the empty chair next to Aunt Shirley. I put my best innocent expression on and waited for his answer.

Garrett paused a little longer before talking. "I can tell you on the record that the Granville Police Department is treating Mr. Manning's death as a homicide."

"How was he killed?" I asked before Aunt Shirley could jump in and divulge what we knew. "Was it poison like we thought? The poison that Sheri admitted to ordering?"

Garrett narrowed his eyes at me. "You know I'm not going to tell you anything pertinent to this investigation. Just know that we are treating his death as a homicide. When I have anything further to discuss, I'll call the paper and let you know."

Aunt Shirley snorted. "Like heck you will. We had to chase you down here just to get confirmation on how you were treating his death."

Garrett gave her a wicked smile but didn't say a word.

Not wanting to be in the middle of World War III, I stood up. While I understood why Garrett had to keep certain information secret, it still made the journalist in me grouchy. "The *Granville Gazette* thanks you for your time, Chief Kimble."

Garrett lifted his eyebrow at the mention of his title. He didn't miss my little tantrum. "Does it now? Well, Sin, I thank you for your time." He walked over to the door and opened it…signaling the end of our meeting.

Aunt Shirley huffed the whole way through the door. As I went to walk through, Garrett grabbed hold of my arm and leaned down to nuzzle my neck.

I melted.

"Be safe today," he whispered. His lips grazed my ear before he kissed my neck.

"C'mon." Aunt Shirley grabbed me and yanked me the rest of the way out the door. "You're a disgrace to your profession, Ryli Jo. This man could sweet talk you into anything."

So true.

Garrett chuckled and I waved goodbye, still feeling the effects of his lips against my ear and neck.

"Are you okay to drive," Aunt Shirley asked snidely as we slid into the Falcon. "Or should I be driving?"

"Oh, hush up. You're just jealous." I pointed the Falcon toward the Manor and tuned Aunt Shirley out.

There was one spot left open in the visitor's parking area. It was almost lunchtime, so that wasn't too big a surprise, especially with Valentine's Day the next day. Family members were coming to spend time with their loved ones.

There was an excitement in the air when we walked inside. Someone had brought out an old record player with records, and a few of the residents were dancing.

"Old Blue Eyes." Aunt Shirley smiled and waved to a group of ladies standing by the albums. "That Frankie sure could sing."

"You miss this place, don't you?"

Aunt Shirley shrugged. "Maybe just a little. Guess not all these old people are awful."

We stopped in front of Sheri Daniels's office door. It was wide open. Not very smart for someone trying to hide something. We slid inside the empty office. I'm not sure what miracle I was hoping for, but I really wanted to find something incriminating. Because like Aunt Shirley, I really didn't want the killer to be Virginia.

"You watch the door," I whispered. "I'll look around on her desk and see if I see anything relevant."

Aunt Shirley huffed. "That used to be my job. Do you even know what you're looking for?"

"Just watch the door."

The truth was I had no idea what I was looking for. Maybe a piece of paper giving step-by-step instructions on how to use the ricin that killed Manning or something along those lines. I rushed over to Sheri's desk and gingerly leafed through some papers. Most were shipping orders for the kitchen. I tried to hide my disappointment.

"Psst. I hear someone." Aunt Shirley motioned me over. We both flattened ourselves against the wall next to the open door. No one would see us as they walked outside in the hallway unless they walked inside the room.

"And he didn't say anything else when he was here this morning?" I recognized the voice as Thomas Shifley's.

"Like what?" Sheri demanded.

"Like for sure how he died," Shifty said impatiently. "Did he tell you that?"

"Why? You know something?" Sheri asked.

"Me? No! Don't you dare try to pin this on me. You have just as much to lose as I do. Even more really. Maybe you're the one that killed him."

Sheri sucked in her breath. "Don't you ever say that out loud again. I didn't kill him. All that Kimble guy said was they were treating the death like a homicide. He told Lucy she couldn't rent out Manning's space yet, and that he'd be back with a search warrant for the Manor."

Garrett had been by this morning?

"I didn't sign up for this," Shifley whined. "I didn't kill anyone."

They walked through the door and into Sheri's room. They still hadn't seen us.

"You sure about that?" Aunt Shirley demanded.

So much for going unnoticed and sneaking out real quick while their backs were turned.

Sheri and Shifley whirled around. Each gave us the stink eye.

"What're you doing in my office uninvited?" Sheri demanded.

Aunt Shirley shrugged. "Just thought we'd come by and say hi. Catch up on old times."

Sheri's face turned red. "Get out, and don't ever come in here again." She hurried over to her desk, looking around frantically. I didn't know if she thought I took something or if she was trying to hide something.

"Let's go," I whispered and tugged on Aunt Shirley's arm.

We scurried to the elevator and got off on Aunt Shirley's floor. There was still yellow tape over Manning's door. I knocked on Virginia's door and waited a few seconds before it was opened.

"Hello ladies," Lovey said. "We're just having a couple celebratory Valentine's Day drinks, won't you join us?"

"You bet," Aunt Shirley said and pushed me aside.

I decided then and there to never stand close to Aunt Shirley when near a moving car or train. She'd push me in front of it just to get to booze.

"It's not Valentine's Day yet," I joked as I followed them inside. *Nor is it even noon yet.*

"That's my fault," Virginia said.

Dotty was in the kitchen putting things away while Virginia was sitting at the table nursing a drink.

"I have a Valentine's Day date tomorrow with Bert, so we decided to have our annual Valentine's Day luncheon and drinks today."

"And now," Dotty announced, "we're gonna top off our day-early Valentine's Day luncheon with my famous Black Forest Manhattan."

"Sounds yummy," Aunt Shirley said. "What's in it?"

"Basically cherry juice, cherry liqueur, whiskey, and chocolate bitters. Very healthy drink."

Lovey and Virginia laughed.

"We've been drinking this drink on Valentine's Day for years," Lovey said. She walked over to the refrigerator and pulled out a jar of cherries. "Then garnish the drink with these bad boys...whiskey soaked cherries."

"But only one for me today," Virginia said. "I want to make sure I'm perky and rested up for my date tomorrow."

I decided I better stop Dotty before she gets out of control with my drink. "Just a tiny shot for me, please. I'm driving today." I turned to Virginia. "What are you doing on your date tomorrow?"

"Well, the Manor is having a movie matinée around two and showing *Pillow Talk* with Doris Day and Rock Hudson."

"That Rock Hudson sure was a hunk," Aunt Shirley said dreamily.

"Yes, he was."

"And Cary Grant."

"And Gregory Peck."

While the ladies tittered and giggled over men I'd never really heard of, Dotty delivered our Black Forest Manhattans to the table. I took a tiny sip as the others all plopped whiskey-soaked cherries in their drinks.

"Then after that, there's dancing in the ballroom, and then the cafeteria is having a Valentine's dinner of Salisbury steak, mashed potatoes, and chocolate dipped strawberries for dessert. It should be a blast."

It actually did sound like fun.

"That's why," Virginia said, "I want to take it easy today and rest up. I want to be in tip-top shape for tomorrow."

I knew my time was coming to an end, so if I wanted to ask Virginia about Manning, I'd have to do it soon. The thing was, I didn't want to upset her. I really couldn't see her being the murderer. But then again, I'd been fooled so many times before.

I took a deep breath. "Did you know Manning's death has been ruled a murder?"

CHAPTER 18

"A murder?" Lovey asked. "You're sure?"

"Yep," Aunt Shirley said. "Got official word this morning from Chief Kimble to put in the paper that it's been ruled a homicide."

"Wow," Virginia said. "I can't believe that. I mean, he wasn't exactly liked, but I can't believe someone would kill him."

"How did he die? Do you know?" Dotty asked. "Was it the ricin thing?"

I didn't want to overplay my hand. "I'm not sure, but since it's being ruled a homicide I'd say it was the ricin."

"That's terrible." Virginia finished off the last of her drink. "He must have been in a lot of pain."

"I guess so," I said. "Can I ask you a question, Virginia?"

Virginia looked surprised. "Of course."

"Did you write a threatening note to Mr. Manning?"

Virginia's mouth dropped open. "How did you know?"

I knew I had to tread lightly. "Just something in passing that was said."

"Oh dear," Lovey said, twisting her hands. "Maybe sending him that letter wasn't such a good idea after all."

"What letter?" Aunt Shirley demanded.

"I may have slipped a note under Manning's door recently after a few drinks with the girls." Virginia put a hand to her chest. "Am I a suspect?"

"I'm sure you're not," I lied. "There are far more guilty people running around this place than you."

Dotty sniffed. "I'd think so. They should be looking at Sheri Daniels or Thomas Shifley before they thought to look at Virginia. We were just getting Mr. Manning back for the threatening notes he sent Virginia."

I nodded. "I understand. I've been thinking about those chocolate covered espresso beans he was always eating. Do you think someone could have done something to those?"

"Poisoned his chocolate?" Virginia asked. "How?"

"I don't know," I said. "I was just brainstorming aloud."

Aunt Shirley took one of her whiskey soaked cherries out of her drink and ate it. "Where did he get his stash from, do you know?"

The three ladies looked at each other. Finally Lovey spoke. "Well, I don't know for sure, but I'd say Sheri Daniels. Manning couldn't run a computer, so he couldn't order them himself. Sheri and Kaylee Jones deal with placing orders for folks here at the Manor."

I was at a loss as to how to trip up Virginia into admitting she doctored the chocolate.

"Did you guys see anyone visit Manning Friday night after Aunt Shirley and I left?" I asked.

Lovey and Dotty exchanged horrified looks.

"Well," Lovey said and slowly raised her hand. "We did. After the altercation in the hall, Dotty and I decided it would be rude seeing as how we are the hospitality team to just leave him in misery. Not so much because we cared about him—but because we didn't want others to whisper about us not doing our job. So we heated up some canned soup and took it over to him. The funny thing is he actually let us inside. We knew then he must be pretty sick. Usually when we stop by he'd slam the door in our faces. But that night he let us in. We set the soup down on the counter and then let ourselves out. I didn't see anyone else around his place later that night, did you Dotty?"

Dotty shook her head. "I sure didn't."

I turned to Virginia. "What about you, Virginia? Did you see anything or anyone suspicious that night? I know you were still out when I came to pick up Aunt Shirley."

Virginia pursed her lips in thought. "Let's see. I got in that night around eight from my date. Bert and I sat downstairs in the main lobby area next to the fireplace and talked for hours after our dinner in the Manor cafeteria. He walked me upstairs to my door and I went inside. We didn't see anyone in the halls during that time."

I thought back to what I'd read online about ricin poison. It could take anywhere from six hours to a couple days for symptoms to become fatal. Maybe I needed to go back and rethink my timeline of where everyone was and who had motive.

I finished off the Black Forest Manhattan, which really was amazing, and pushed back my chair. "I basically wanted to stop by, Virginia, to remind you your article will be in the *Gazette* tomorrow morning."

Virginia clapped her hands together. "Thank you, dear. I can't wait to read it."

They walked Aunt Shirley and me to the door, and we said our goodbyes. I was stalling because I just knew I was missing something.

"The last time we all saw Manning before he got sick," I said. "When would you say that was?"

Lovey looked up in thought then turned to the other ladies. "I'd say it was last Thursday—after the interview. I remember we had just shut the door, and a few seconds later we heard the commotion in the hallway. Manning and Mr. Shifley were out here, and we interrupted the fight between Manning and Shirley. Do you guys remember that?"

Virginia nodded. "Yes. Manning had threatened to get Shirley kicked out and Shirley had threatened to shove those chocolate covered espresso beans down his throat."

The ladies all snickered—including Aunt Shirley.

Once again I was back to square one with either Sheri Daniels or Thomas Shifley as the killer...with a possible motive of Manning being able to identify the Manor thief as the catalyst.

We said goodbye to the girls and headed to the elevator.

"We need to find Kaylee and talk with her," Aunt Shirley said when we got in the elevator.

I looked at the clock on my cell phone. "Wonder where she eats lunch?"

"There's a lounge outside the cafeteria for the workers. Let's start there."

The Manor cafeteria was in full swing for lunch. Dozens of residents were milling around the tables, some talking, some eating. A few of them called out to us as we made our way toward the employee lounge.

I pushed open the lounge door and walked in. There were about twelve workers eating their lunch at the round tables in the workroom. There were three vending machines lined against a wall, one selling sandwiches, apples, yogurt, and candy, another selling soft drinks, and another one selling different types of coffee.

A bald-headed burly man looked up from his meal when we opened the lounge door and walked through. "Hey, you two can't be back here." He stood up. His broad upper torso and massive arm muscles flexed. I saw the bottom half of a tattoo peek out of his shirt uniform. I definitely didn't want to catch this guy in a dark alley.

Aunt Shirley whipped something out of her coat pocket so fast it left me dizzy. "This is official newspaper business. My badge here says I'm with the media. You go back to your lunch and no one will get hurt."

Big Baldy looked momentarily confused. He looked back and forth between us, then shrugged his massive shoulders and went back to his lunch. I blew out the breath I'd been holding.

"I see her," Aunt Shirley said and tugged on my arm.

"Since when do we have official media badges?"

Aunt Shirley grinned. "Since I printed one off the Internet a few weeks ago."

Kaylee Jones was methodically pulling the crust off her sandwich when we pulled out the two empty chairs on either side of her. Her straight brown hair fell over her eyes and covered most of her face. She looked tired and miserable. I instantly felt horrible that someone this young would be shrouded in this much sadness.

"Mind if we sit down?" I asked.

She shrugged but didn't say anything.

"My name is Ryli, and this is Aunt Shirley. And we were—"

"I know who you are and why you're here," Kaylee whispered. "Please just leave me alone."

Aunt Shirley leaned closer to Kaylee. "We just have a couple questions we'd like to ask you."

Kaylee chucked her half-eaten sandwich onto the table, lifted her head up, and looked frantically around the room. She stuck her thumbnail in her mouth and started to nibble.

142

"I'll tell you the same thing I told the cops. I don't know nothin' about the stolen boxes out of the pantry or the stolen items from the residents' rooms."

Oh, I think you do.

I leaned toward her. "I'm just curious about the shipment that was stolen from the pantry. Were you the one that placed the order?"

"Sheri did," Kaylee said.

"But you were the one that moved the boxes to the pantry?" I asked.

Tiny nod from Kaylee.

"Who else knew about the order?" I asked. "Do you know?"

Kaylee shrugged. "I don't know. Anyone could have. It's not like I hide the purchase orders. Plus, all the departments had to tell me what they wanted. For instance, food service told me they needed the utensils and napkins, and health service told me what medications they needed. I got the order for castor beans and the other herbs from the greenhouse."

"Who's in charge of ordering for the greenhouse?" I asked.

Kaylee's eyes grew big and she shook her head. "I can't tell you." She looked around the lounge again. "Please, I already have the chief guy mad at me. He's threatened to haul me in, but I just can't."

"Is it your baby you're worried about?" Aunt Shirley asked. "I know you have a new one to look after."

Tears filled Kaylee's eyes. "Please," she whispered. "I can't help you. I *need* this job. I'll do whatever it takes to keep this job."

I actually hated myself for what I was about to do.

"And I believe you," I said. "Want to know why? Because I heard you threaten to kill Ray Manning the other day. I was hiding behind the door when you two got into an altercation in the hallway."

Huge, silent tears fell from Kaylee's eyes. It was kinda eerie how she could cry without making a sound. Aunt Shirley reached over and removed a couple napkins from the dispenser on the table and handed them to Kaylee.

"I promise whatever you tell us," Aunt Shirley whispered, "will stay between us. No one has to know you ever said a thing. The police would have to go about legal channels, which may come back on you. But we don't have to do that. You tell us something and we'll take care of it on our own."

Jeez, she makes us sound like we're the Mafia now!

Kaylee tucked her head down again so her hair was hiding her face. "You promise you won't bring me into this?"

"You have my word," Aunt Shirley said solemnly.

Kaylee swiped at her nose with the wadded up napkins in her hand. "I honestly have no idea why Ray Manning was killed. I don't know if he was involved with the people who are stealing from the residents or not, or if he stumbled upon who they were and that's why he was killed."

"Do you know who's stealing from the residents?" I asked.

Kaylee's nod was barely noticeable. "I've been watching closely the last few days. I may know at least one person involved."

Aunt Shirley and I leaned in as close as we could to her. I could feel my heart pounding in my chest. I looked up and caught the eye of Big Baldy. He was facing our table and seemed to be watching us with too much interest.

Fearing for Kaylee's safety more than her job, I decided a distraction was in order. I stood up from the table, rummaged around in my pockets for change, and walked toward Big Baldy and the coffee machine. I knew Aunt Shirley had it under control with Kaylee.

Big Baldy watched me stroll toward the coffee machine—his eyes never leaving me. I could feel my legs getting weaker the closer I got to him. My fingers were shaking as I put the thirty-five cents into the machine. I have no idea what number I pushed, but it must have been right because the cup plopped down and a few seconds later thick, black coffee dispersed.

I reached down to get the coffee and saw Big Baldy stand up and walk over to me. My mouth felt like the Sahara Desert, and I forgot how to breathe.

He didn't stop…just slowed down long enough to throw away his trash in the receptacle next to me. I didn't have to wait long before he opened his mouth and spoke. "Leave it be."

CHAPTER 19

"So Sheri Daniels is in charge of purchase orders for the greenhouse, and Thomas Shifley is one of the people she thinks is stealing from the residents," I said. I can't say I was too shocked to find out Shifley was involved with stealing from the residents.

Aunt Shirley nodded. "Now all we need to do is prove it's Sheri Daniels that Shifty's working with, find the stolen goods, and then prove Sheri Daniels is the killer."

I chuckled at Aunt Shirley's optimism.

We stopped to zip up our coats in front of the Manor door.

"Move it."

I looked up and saw Carl Baker push his way through us. I looked at Aunt Shirley and saw the light bulb go on for her, too.

We waited until he got far enough ahead before we took off after him—being sure to stay out of sight. We caught him going through the Tropical Paradise double doors.

I peeked through one of the windows on the swinging doors and saw Baker talking with Shifley. I motioned for Aunt Shirley to have a look for herself in the other window.

I couldn't hear what they were saying, but the animation let me know they were both pretty angry.

Aunt Shirley ducked back out of sight and I followed suit.

"So do you think it's just Baker and Shifley?" I asked. "Or do you think it's Baker, Shifley, and Sheri Daniels involved with the stolen goods?"

Aunt Shirley shook her head. "I have no idea. We need to get into Shifley's house just to make sure he has the stolen items on him."

"We need to tell Garrett what we know," I countered.

146

Aunt Shirley scowled at me. "He'll figure it out on his own. This is for us and the *Gazette* readers."

I wasn't sure I agreed with a word she said, but I let it go. She was right, Garrett was probably already on it. He'd surely put the pieces together before us.

We made a quick stop at Burger Barn to grab burgers and fries before heading back to the office. It was a late lunch, but better late than never when it came to food.

I was surprised to see Paige's Tahoe parked in the parking lot. Until I remembered tomorrow was Valentine's Day! With the discovery of the body and trying to solve the case, I'd completely forgotten. We'd made plans last week to go shopping and buy our guys gifts today.

Mindy was sitting at her desk leafing through a magazine and laughing with Paige when we strolled in. Paige was sitting at my desk.

I plopped the burgers down and started dispensing while Aunt Shirley went to grab Cokes from the refrigerator.

"I'm so sorry, Paige," I said as I handed Mindy a cheeseburger. "I totally forgot you were coming by. Do you want half my cheeseburger?"

Paige shook her head. "No, thanks. I had lunch before I left the house."

"It won't take us long to eat," I said. "Then we can head out."

"So what did you learn?" Mindy asked as she munched on a greasy fry.

Aunt Shirley plunked down a can of soda in front of each of us. "That Thomas Shifley is stealing from the residents. We just need to figure out who all is working with him. He and Sheri

Daniels are now my number one suspects for the Manning murder."

"Did you notice the big, scary bald guy in the lounge?" I asked Aunt Shirley.

"Yep. Definitely looked like he could hold his own in a fight. What? You think he's involved?"

"Well, I noticed him watching us. So I went to go get a coffee, and when he got up to throw away his trash he told me to 'leave it be,' then walked away."

"Sounds scary," Paige said. "Please be careful. I feel like I say this a lot with you two, but please don't do anything foolish."

Aunt Shirley laughed. "We have jobs to do. People in this town have a right to know what's going on and we're the ones to expose it!"

I wasn't quite sure about all that. "I feel better knowing we at least have a motive if Shifley turns out to be the murderer."

"Where are you girls off to today?" Mindy asked as she wadded up her wrapper and placed it in the Burger Barn bag.

"Need to go to Brywood to pick the guys up a couple Valentine's Day gifts," I said. "Then head over to Cellar Ridge Winery to pick up a bottle of Scully's White to drink with the romantic Valentine's meal Garrett and I are having."

Mindy smiled. "Sounds nice. I already got my gift. You want to see it?"

A Valentine's Day gift for a seasoned Marine who cusses like a sailor and chews on the end of cigars all day…couldn't wait to see this gift.

Aunt Shirley clapped her hands together. "Let's see what you got the curmudgeon."

We all laughed and Mindy looked over her shoulder to make sure Hank wasn't around. She opened the bottom of a deep-set filing cabinet and took out a box. She set it on the desk and took one more look over her shoulder.

"He ain't coming," Aunt Shirley assured her. "Let's see it."

Mindy reached in and lifted out a beautiful lamp. On closer inspection, it wasn't just any old lamp, it was a table lamp made for a Marine. The bulk of the lamp had the Eagle, Globe, and Anchor emblem of the Corps sitting on a wooden base with the words Semper Fi inscribed on a brass plaque. There was a tiny fabric flag perched on top next to the pull-down lever to turn on the lamp. The lampshade had the colors of the Corps—scarlet, blue, and gold—with the values Honor, Courage, and Commitment written in gold along the base of the blue shade.

Tears filled my eyes. "Omigosh, Mindy. You did great with this gift. He'll love it."

Mindy wiped the tears from her cheeks. "I think so, too. I really wanted to do something special for him this year. It's thirty-five years ago this year that he enlisted and went to boot camp. I just wanted to honor him for that."

Aunt Shirley sniffed and wiped her nose. "Well, it's more than that old grouch deserves. Ryli's right, you did good with this."

I smiled at Mindy. "He's so lucky to have you."

"And I'm lucky to have him."

Paige reached across and hugged Mindy. "I hope thirty-five years from now I'm doing romantic things like this for Matt."

"What in tarnation is going on out here?" Hank bellowed from his office door.

We all screamed and stood behind Mindy so she could quickly put the gift away before Hank saw.

Hank scowled at us. "I don't pay you to stand around and hug and cry and sing *Kumbaya*. I pay you to get me stories."

Mindy closed the file cabinet drawer as Hank walked over to the desk. "And what is this one doing here?" He took the cigar out of his mouth and waved it around Paige. "She doesn't work here now, too, does she? Did she get put on the payroll?"

"Simmer down, cupcake," Aunt Shirley said. "We just got back from questioning our leads in the Manning murder, and now we're heading out to get some quotes."

We were?

"Well, what're you standing around here for?" Hank grumbled. "Go do some interviews."

I grinned, grabbed my coat, and motioned for Aunt Shirley and Paige. "On it, boss. See ya tomorrow."

"Hold up," Hank said. "You're telling me it's going to take you the rest of the day to do an interview?"

"Hank." Mindy laid her hand on his arm. "Let the girls do their jobs. They've never let us down before."

I blew her a kiss and we scurried out the door and piled into the Falcon.

"Just once I think we need to take my car," Paige pouted from the backseat as she zipped up her black jacket. "The heater works great and –"

"Not gonna happen," Aunt Shirley said.

CHAPTER 20

Cellar Ridge Winery was located off the beaten path about fifteen minutes between Granville and Brywood. The wood, earth tones, and stone both inside and out gave the winery a Tuscany feel.

We decided to have a glass of wine and sit by the fireplace. We weren't in that big of a hurry. After we paid for our drinks and four bottles of wine, we headed to Brywood to get gifts for Matt and Garrett.

"I still can't believe you bought a bottle of wine, Aunt Shirley." She hardly ever drank wine. In fact, the last time I tried to give her white wine at Paige's bachelorette party, she vowed to disown me.

"You got a bottle for your beau, Paige got a bottle for her and Matt, and your mom got a bottle for her and Doc. I figured at this rate if I get me a bottle maybe I'll get lucky and get me a beau that night. After all, I'll be all alone, by myself, no one to share it with."

I knew she said the last part just to make me feel guilty—and it succeeded. But not guilty enough that I was willing to let her tag along on my date with Garrett.

"Maybe it will," Paige said diplomatically. She knew what Aunt Shirley was trying to do, and she wasn't having it.

Aunt Shirley huffed, crossed her arms, looked out the window and pouted.

"Why don't you ask Old Man Jenkins what he's doing tomorrow night?" I suggested. "Maybe you can do the same date Virginia and Bert are doing."

Aunt Shirley pouted even more—if that's possible. "He should be asking me. I shouldn't have to do the asking."

I rolled my eyes at her logic.

"Do you know what you're getting Matt?" I asked, hoping to steer the conversation elsewhere.

"He really wants a Zero Tolerance knife," Paige said. "So I guess I'm going with that."

"I'm getting Garrett a Benchmade knife."

Aunt Shirley turned to face us. "Well, I'm getting myself a pair of nunchucks."

Paige and I laughed.

"No, you aren't," I chided.

"Yes, I am. I've been watching these YouTube videos on how to use them."

I groaned. "What do you need nunchucks for?"

"There's a killer running around loose. I may be attacked and need to defend myself."

"With nunchucks?" I saw nothing good coming from this.

I pulled the Falcon into the parking lot of Locked & Loaded. This was my first time here. But I'd heard Matt and Garrett talk about it so much I knew the people inside would take good care of me.

A doorbell sounded as we walked in the store. It was very intimidating. There were guns of all sizes and makes hanging on the walls. I'm not really a gun person. I do know the difference between a rifle and a pistol, but that's about all.

Aunt Shirley did have a snub-nose revolver that she liked to carry. But pulling it out one too many times on innocent citizens, Garrett finally confiscated it. Now she was into her blowgun…and apparently nunchucks.

A tall, dark-haired gentleman about sixty years old walked out from behind a curtain from the back. He had brown eyes and a pencil-thin mustache. His face lit up when he saw Aunt Shirley. "Well, now, look who's here? It's my favorite customer. I almost didn't recognize you with your new hair. It's gorgeous. But you always are."

Aunt Shirley preened. "Delbert, you old charmer you. How you been?"

"Pretty good. I'd be doing better if you married me."

My mouth dropped open. This dude was hitting on Aunt Shirley?

"Close your mouth, flies will get in." Aunt Shirley nudged me aside and sashayed to the counter. "Now you know I can't go and marry you, Delbert. What would my other boyfriends think?"

Delbert placed his hand over his heart. "They'd think I was one lucky son of a gun. No pun intended."

I rolled my eyes at Paige. "Ahem. Aunt Shirley, if we can tear you two lovebirds away, we need to get the gifts and head on back."

Delbert clapped his hands together. "Is this your great-niece, Ryli, I've heard so much about?" He rushed around the counter and took my hand in his. He brought it up to his mouth and kissed the back of my hand.

Yuck.

I tried surreptitiously to wipe my hand on my jeans. I didn't want to offend the guy, but...yuck!

"That's her," Aunt Shirley said. "She and I are living together now for a while."

"You lucky girl. I'd give anything to be able to live with your Aunt Shirley."

I perked up. "Really? Because for about fifty bucks I can let you have her."

Delbert threw back his head and laughed. "Oh, you silly girl. You really are a kidder."

"Actually I'm not," I insisted. "You can really have her."

Paige giggled but grabbed hold of my arm. "Yes, she's a kidder our Ryli."

Delbert smiled at Paige. "And you must be the lovely bride of Matt's." He looked down at her flat belly. "I hear we're still waiting for the next Sinclair heir."

Paige's mouth dropped open.

I couldn't help but laugh at this guy's audacity. Who was he? Was he stalking my family? How the heck did he know so much about us?

Delbert must have read my thoughts. "Your aunt keeps us all informed on her Facebook page."

I heard Paige suck in her breath and knew we needed to get on with the knife buying. Or maybe not. At this rate, Paige may shank Aunt Shirley in the parking lot.

"So what can I do for you ladies today?" Delbert asked. "Another blowgun for you, Shirley?"

"So you're the one to blame for that, huh?" I asked.

Delbert laughed. "I thought it would be right up her alley."

154

"And it is," Aunt Shirley agreed. "I use it all the time."

"So if not a blowgun, what then?" Delbert asked.

We spent the next twenty minutes looking at knives. By the time Delbert was done showing us his collection, I felt I knew everything there was to ever know about knives. I couldn't wait to regurgitate my new information to Garrett and impress him with my knowledge.

Paige and I picked out the merchandise we wanted and paid for the items.

"What about you, beautiful? What can I interest you in today?"

Aunt Shirley grinned. "I want some nunchucks."

Delbert clapped his hands together. "The nunchaku. A traditional Okinawan martial arts weapon. Good choice! You will not be disappointed. Come, come."

He ushered us over to a display case.

"I thought they were called nunchucks," I said.

Delbert shook his head. "They are actually called nunchaku, but people often say nunchucks." He pulled out a pair that had two wooden handles and a chain hooking them together. He handed them to Aunt Shirley. "Make sure it's a good length. Hold one handle in your hand and drape it up your arm and to your shoulder." She grabbed one handle and did what he said. She then held on to one handle and let the other side dangle, moving her wrist slowly back and forth.

"They got a good feel," Aunt Shirley said. "I'll take them."

Delbert wiggled his eyebrows at her. "You need me to show you how to use those?"

Gag!

"Maybe someday," Aunt Shirley said. "Right now I'm focused on catching us a killer."

Delbert perked up. "Oh, really. I hadn't heard about a murder in Granville. What happened?"

Aunt Shirley's eyes lit up. "My neighbor at the Manor, Ray Manning, was poisoned."

"You don't say," Delbert said. "Any suspects yet?"

Aunt Shirley scoffed. "Well, outside of me…yes, we got a few. I'm fairly certain Sheri Daniels or Thomas Shifley is the killer. Now it's just a matter of pinning down which one."

"I don't think I know this Sheri Daniels or Thomas Shifley," Delbert said. "You girls be careful now. You sure you don't need another gun?"

"No!" Paige and I exclaimed at the same time.

Delbert looked lewdly at Aunt Shirley. "Well, if you change your mind, you know where to find me."

Paige and I dragged Aunt Shirley out of Locked & Loaded before she came home with anything more dangerous than the nunchucks. And, yes, I included Delbert in that little scenario.

By the time we got back to Granville, it was a little after four. I dropped Paige off at the office so she could get her Tahoe and head home. I could see Mindy inside on the phone talking excitedly to someone. I immediately felt guilty for leaving her all day.

"Let's go in real quick and see if she needs anything."

Aunt Shirley sighed. "Fine. But then I need to get home and relax. I've had a hard day."

"We haven't done anything," I said dryly.

"Exactly. Which is why I'm tired. Had we actually accomplished something today, like chase a bad guy, I'd be good to go."

I kept repeating to myself that as soon as I solved this case, Aunt Shirley was back at the Manor. I had an end in sight. I just had to keep my eye on the prize.

Mindy saw us and waved us over. We both sat down at our desks and waited for Mindy to finish her call. "Okay, thanks for the info. I'll talk with you later." She hung up the phone and gave a girly squeal. "I have it on very good authority that Garrett executed two search warrants today. One for Oak Grove Manor's files, *and* a search warrant for Sheri Daniels's house!"

I gasped. I guess I shouldn't be surprised that Garrett would think to search Sheri's home. After all he's the professional. Or so he keeps telling me.

"I wonder what new evidence arose for search warrants to be served at her personal house?" I asked.

Aunt Shirley frowned. "I told you we should have searched her bedroom! Now Garrett will get the credit and we'll have to get the story from him."

I only heard one thing...an arrest was imminent, and Aunt Shirley was out of my hair! "Guess you can go back home," I said, trying to contain my excitement so I didn't hurt her feelings.

Aunt Shirley squinted at me. "Not quite. They still have to find the stolen items, link her to Manning's murder, and officially arrest her first. Which probably won't happen until tomorrow or Wednesday at the latest. They still have to find enough evidence to hold her."

I threw up my hands. "I thought you said she did it!"

"I said *maybe* she did it. Maybe. I don't go home until the killer is captured. Period. I'm not gonna be no sitting duck in my apartment, waiting for a killer to come get me."

I sighed and rolled my eyes at Mindy.

"I can see you, you ninny!" Aunt Shirley exclaimed.

Plop! Plop!

I took out my cell phone and read the message from Garrett. "He says he's pretty sure I've already heard about the search warrants. He won't be home until late. He'll call me tonight if it's not too late. Otherwise he'll see me tomorrow."

"Guess there's nothing else more for us to do," Aunt Shirley said. "Let's go home and make an early night of it."

Great, just what I wanted to do…make an early night of it with Aunt Shirley. I was too young to make an early night of it. Even though it's what I usually did most nights.

Miss Molly was howling her displeasure at the world in general when I opened my front door and went inside. "I'm coming. I'm coming."

"I'm going to go change into something more comfortable," Aunt Shirley said and made a beeline for my bedroom.

I opened a can of cat food and put it in Miss Molly's pink, diamond-encrusted bowl. She nudged my hand out of the way and started purring and eating.

"I'll warm us up some soup," I yelled out to Aunt Shirley.

"Sounds good."

I'd just ladled the soup in the bowls when Aunt Shirley walked into the kitchen and handed me a tube. "Ya know, I just don't understand this lip stuff you have. I've been putting it on for a couple days now, and I don't think it works at all."

It was my extremely expensive lip cream for preventative wrinkles around my lips. It cost an equivalent of what I make in one day working at the *Gazette*. "Where have you been putting this?" I was almost afraid of her answer.

"On my lips. It says it's lip cream. But it's only made my lips really super dry and chapped."

I didn't know whether to strangle her for wasting such an expensive tube of makeup, or laugh at the fact she thought lip cream went *on* the lips like Carmex.

I sighed and handed the depleted tube back to her. "You're supposed to put it *around* your lips to prevent fine lines and wrinkles."

Aunt Shirley cackled and hit me on my arm. "A little too late for me. I have about a hundred wrinkles around my lips. But that makes sense now as to why it was drying my lips out." She flipped the tube over in her hands. "I bet this stuff works pretty good for people your age. You may have to buy another tube, though. Hope it wasn't too expensive."

I counted to ten and prayed not only that there was still some cream left in the tube, but that someone would solve this case soon so Aunt Shirley could go back to her own place. I wasn't sure how much more my sanity could take.

Mom called around eight, and I was glad for the distraction. I was curious how Garrett was coming on Sheri's house. Did he find any stolen items? Would he arrest her immediately for the thefts or would he wait and build a case for Manning's murder, also? If he arrested her immediately, I was anxious to hear what his motive was.

When nine o'clock came and went and I still hadn't heard from Garrett, I decided to put down the book I was pretending to read and call it a night. Tomorrow was a new day...Valentine's Day.

CHAPTER 21

"I took the liberty of ordering us matching Valentine's Day sweatshirts," Aunt Shirley said from inside the bathroom.

No way was I going to be her Bobbsey Twin today. "Didn't you just get a Valentine's Day sweater? You remember, that disastrous thing you wore the other day to church."

I heard the toilet flush and Aunt Shirley opened the door. "These are waaaay better."

I motioned for her to come out so I could go in. "Great, can't wait." I closed the door and leaned against it. The last three days, this was the only place in my house I could get privacy. How sad was that?

I finished using the bathroom and walked out into my tiny dressing area. Aunt Shirley thrust a sweatshirt at me and grinned. I was immediately on guard.

"I'm not so sure about us dressing alike," I said. I didn't want to hurt her feelings, but it just wasn't happening.

Aunt Shirley pouted. "I did buy me a backup sweatshirt just in case you threw a big baby fit."

"Good."

Aunt Shirley waved her arms at me. "Open it up."

I held my breath as I slowly unfolded the pink sweatshirt. I read it and laughed. It was actually quite funny. It was a voter's ballot. There was an empty box for Taken, an empty box for Single, and a checkmark in the box for Who Cares I'm Awesome!

"I actually like it a lot." I loved the soft feel of the sweatshirt and the fact it had an extra-wide neck opening, for a sexy collarbone exposure and cleavage look. "I'll be happy to wear it. But only me. You wear the other one." I've seen Aunt Shirley undressed, and believe me no one wanted to see her wrinkled cleavage today.

"Fine. I'll be right out. Then we can head to the office."

I paired my new pink sweatshirt with black skinny jeans and black Converse. Cute, yet comfortable enough to chase down a story and a killer if need be. Very practical.

While Aunt Shirley finished getting dressed, I made us coffees to go. No offense to Mindy, but she was just going to have tea at the office. I needed something with a little more kick this morning. Kick in the shape of caffeine and chocolate.

"Okay," Aunt Shirley said as she walked into the living room. "I'm ready."

I almost choked on the coffee I'd just swallowed. Why? Why couldn't she just wear something cute like what I had on? Instead, she had on a pair of red polyester pants with a black sweatshirt that had an image in the center of a large hand holding a gun with the slogan *love kills*. It looked like the gun was pointed right at you.

I shook my head. "Why couldn't you have gotten one that was cute like mine?"

Aunt Shirley lifted her hands in the air and looked down at her shirt. "What? I think it's great because it doubles as a public service announcement."

I closed my eyes. "Fine. Let's go. I don't want to be late. I hate when Hank looks at me all disapprovingly."

I left Miss Molly a full bowl of food in the hopes she wouldn't scream at me when I got home. We each grabbed our coffees and purses and made our way to the Falcon.

"Hey, should we take a selfie of our sweatshirts for the *Gazette* page?" Aunt Shirley asked as I started the car and let it warm up.

"No."

"How about for my personal Facebook page? Maybe we should post it there?"

Instead of answering I pulled the Falcon out of my tiny driveway and headed for the office.

Plop! Plop!

"Check that for me, would you?" I asked.

Aunt Shirley dug around in my purse until she found my cell phone. She swiped it open. "It's Garrett. He basically says good morning, and that he didn't get in until late last night. No arrest has been made yet, but one should be coming soon."

"Darn him for not telling me more! Like did they find any stolen items in Sheri's house?"

Aunt Shirley grinned. "That just means we do a little digging of our own today."

I nodded and smiled. "Deal."

No matter how frustrated I felt sometimes about Aunt Shirley, one thing was certain…together, we made a great team.

I know it seems I'm always bragging about my commute time, but it's true. There's nothing like small-town living when it comes to getting to work in under five minutes.

Mindy was already busy fielding calls when we walked in. She looked adorable in a red sweater with the word "love" written in pink sparkles, red leggings with tiny white hearts, and red open-toed high heels.

I unzipped my coat and hung it up, still wondering how the search warrants came out. I had some contacts I could call, but I had to be careful word wouldn't get back to Garrett. It wasn't always a perk when your boyfriend was the Chief of Police.

Mindy hung up the phone and cheered. "I have great news. But before I tell, let me just say I love the outfits. Ryli, very cute and fitting. And Aunt Shirley, always very fitting."

I smiled at her diplomacy. "Thanks. It was a gift this morning from Aunt Shirley."

"I bought me the same sweatshirt, but the princess here wanted to be the only one wearing that shirt, so I put on my backup."

Hank's door flew open and he strode quickly to our desks. "Did you tell them?"

"Not yet," Mindy said. "I was getting to it."

Hank looked at me, then Aunt Shirley. He grunted. "Ryli, ridiculous shirt. Shirley, love it."

Aunt Shirley grinned at me. I should have known Hank would love her shirt. He probably had one to match at home.

"Okay," Mindy said, taking a sip of her hot tea. "I just got off the phone with one of my contacts at the courthouse, and she claims Garrett is trying to get a search warrant for Thomas Shifley. He hasn't obtained it yet, but it's coming down the pike."

I sucked in my breath and looked at Aunt Shirley wide-eyed. Garrett must be closing in!

Hank yanked the unlit cigar out of his mouth. "Well, what are you two waiting for? Get me a story today. I want this solved by press time next week! That means you have until Thursday to get me something. You got two front-page stories this morning. Get me this and it will be another front-pager for you."

I squealed like a little girl inside my head. I didn't want to give him a reason to roll his eyes in disgust at me. But I was motivated even more now to find the killer. It was one thing to get Aunt Shirley out of my house. It was another to have three front-page stories two weeks in a row.

"Your deadline is Thursday," Hank reminded me. "That gives you two more days to wrap this up."

He turned and walked into his office and slammed the door.

"Have you seen the paper this morning?" Mindy asked.

I grinned. "Nope. I wanted to wait until I got here."

Mindy thrust the paper sitting on her desk at me. I unfolded it and slowly walked to my desk. It felt amazing to see I had two bylines…both on the front page! These weren't fluff pieces I normally write. These were true journalistic articles.

I finished reading, then turned to Aunt Shirley. "Where should we start this morning?"

She pursed her lips in thought. "Let's see if ole Shifty is home or at work."

"You want me to call the Manor for you and ask to speak to him?" Mindy asked.

Aunt Shirley nodded and took out a notepad and pen. "Ryli, start writing down a timeline of his movements that we remember from last Wednesday until Saturday. I'm going to write down questions to ask."

I got busy with the timeline as Mindy called the Manor. From the one-sided conversation it was easy to tell he wasn't at work.

"Seems Thomas Shifley clocked out early yesterday claiming he was sick and has called in sick today," Mindy gleefully informed us.

I put the finishing touches on my timeline of every time I saw Shifley that week, what he was doing, and who he was with.

The three of us spent the next few minutes going over the timeline, questions to ask, and possible motives Shifley had for killing Manning. Everything was in place. All we needed to do was confront him with our information, find the stolen items, and then have him arrested.

"Are you sure you don't want to come with us?" I asked as I stuffed Shifley's address into my coat pocket.

"I better stay back and man the phones. But keep me posted as to what's going on."

I watched as Aunt Shirley flipped up the hood on her camo parka and tied it under her chin.

"Why are you suddenly wearing the hat that goes with the coat?" I asked. "I've never really seen you wear it."

Aunt Shirley managed to look chagrin as she pulled on her gloves. "Maybe this hairstyle should have waited until summer. Lately one side of my head has been really cold."

By the time I stopped laughing, my side hurt and I was bent over trying to ease the pain. I was glad she saw how ridiculous the hairstyle was. That kind of style didn't even look good on young emo kids. It was hideous.

"It's not *that* funny," Aunt Shirley sniffed.

"Yeah, kinda it is. I tried to tell you, but you wouldn't listen."

She flipped me the bird. Or at least I'm assuming she did. I couldn't really tell with all the padding around her fingers from the gloves.

"You two girls be careful," Mindy called out to us.

I was heading for the door when the flower shop truck pulled up and parked. Nancy Sellers got out carrying two bouquets of roses. My heart raced. I was sure one had to be from Garrett.

"Happy Valentine's Day, ladies," Nancy said cheerfully. "Got deliveries for Mindy and Ryli."

Mindy and I squealed and ran to her. She gave us each our flowers, then waved goodbye.

My hand was shaking when I read the card. It was from Garrett with a promise of a wonderful night, and that he couldn't wait to see me.

"Hank, he always remembers." Mindy wiped tears from her eyes and looked at Hank's door. I don't know how he knew, but he chose that moment to open his door and lean against the door frame.

"You're my rock." He winked at Mindy and then slammed his door shut.

"He's such a romantic," she gushed.

Whatever you say.

I put the roses on my desk and smelled them one last time.

"I suppose those are from lover boy?" Aunt Shirley asked. "Is he covering his bases tonight on getting lucky?"

I ignored her remark, walked out the door, and started up the Falcon. I wasn't going to let her take this moment from me.

Thomas Shifley lived in town over on Willow Street, right behind the grocery store. I pulled the Falcon into his driveway and scrunched my nose at the outside of his small, two-story house. "He's not fencing the stolen items and using the money to clean up his place, that's for sure."

Aunt Shirley chuckled and agreed with me.

The outside of his house looked like it hadn't seen a power washer…ever. There were streaks of black and green on the white exterior. He'd stapled clear plastic over his windows to try and keep the heat in and the cold out. I wasn't holding my breath that it was doing any good because most of the plastic tarps had holes in them.

Aunt Shirley and I sloshed through the snow that still covered his walkway and knocked the snow off our shoes the best we could. Obviously, I hadn't thought I'd be trudging through snow when I put my shoes on this morning. Now my feet were soaking wet and freezing.

I raised my hand and knocked loudly on the door. A few seconds later Thomas Shifley swung the door open. A bottle was hanging from his hand, and a semi-drunken sneer was plastered on his face.

"I ought to kill you both right now," Shifty said.

168

CHAPTER 22

I was thinking of telling Shifley we'd come back later, when Aunt Shirley suddenly pushed on my back and propelled me inside the house.

Aunt Shirley put her hands on her hips. "Save the theatrics for later, Shifty. We're here on important newspaper business."

He narrowed his eyes at us. "Whaddaya mean?"

Aunt Shirley scoffed. "Please, you don't expect us to believe you killed Manning, do you?"

We don't?

Sometimes I get so confused with Aunt Shirley's thinking. I can never tell if she's serious, using reverse psychology, or using serious reverse-psychology...if that's even a thing.

I unzipped my jacket, hung it over my arm, and sat down gingerly on the edge of Shifley's stained couch. No way was I sitting down on his filthy couch in my new coat. God only knows what the stains were from, and I wasn't about to ask.

Shifley plopped down on a recliner that looked like it had seen its best day years ago. "Whaddya want?" He took a swig straight from the bottle then wiped his mouth with the back of his hand.

Aunt Shirley unzipped her coat and sat down on the stained couch next to me. "Just a few questions. First off, I'm assuming Chief Kimble has talked to you about the stolen goods and Manning's death?"

"Duh."

"Have you spoken with Sheri today?" Aunt Shirley asked.

"No." Shifley took another swig. At this rate he'd have about two more questions in him before he passed out. "Why would I want to talk with anyone from that place?"

From his cavalier attitude, I figured he didn't have any idea that Sheri had been served warrants last night or that Garrett was trying to get a search warrant for his place. Which was probably a good thing for us.

"Do you know anything about the stolen items and burglary ring that's going on at the Manor?" I asked.

Shifley shook his head. "Of course not. I have nothing to do with that. If anyone told you otherwise—they're a liar!"

I was willing to bet Kaylee was telling the truth over Shifley, but I wasn't going to press the issue.

Shifty belched. "That witch Sheri Daniels has it in for me, that's all. She's trying to pin everything on me!"

Aunt Shirley leaned forward on the couch, her body moving closer to Shifley's. "Let me ask you…do you think Sheri killed Manning?"

Shifley shrugged. "I dunno. Everybody hated the guy." Shifley took another drink and looked at Aunt Shirley over the bottle. He finished drinking and wiped his mouth. "Heck, at one point I figured you killed him." I could tell he was beginning to slow down by the way his eyes were drooping. Next would be the slurred speech.

Aunt Shirley nodded. "You're right. I did my fair share of threatening him."

"Darn right you did." Another drink. Then another belch. "Anything else? I need to rest my eyes. Room's beginning to spin a little."

Aunt Shirley smiled. "Just one more question. Did you kill Manning?"

My eyes darted to Aunt Shirley. What was she thinking asking a drunk, angry man a question like that!

"Get out!" Shifley tried to stand, but the room must have been spinning more than he suspected because he landed with a soft thud back down on the recliner. He lowered his chin to his chest, his mouth hanging open, closed his eyes, and started to snore.

"This is creepy," I said. "What do we do now?"

Aunt Shirley smiled. "I couldn't have planned this better myself."

I suppressed a groan. "What do you mean?"

"I mean now we have plenty of time to look around and see if we find a clue that tells us whether or not he killed Manning, or whether or not he has stolen property in his possession. I'd bet anything he's good for one of those dastardly deeds."

"What are we looking for? An empty package of castor seeds and melted chocolate?" I asked snidely. "Do you really think he'd just leave them or any of the stolen items out in plain view?"

"Look at him. He's passed out in a drunken stupor before lunch. He's not exactly a genius."

Good point.

"Fine," I sighed. "I'll take the kitchen and you…"

I trailed off because Aunt Shirley was already heading upstairs. "I'm going to see what this freak keeps in his bedroom. I just hope it's not too crazy, even for me."

With one last look at the snoring body, I heaved myself up off the couch and gingerly made my way to the kitchen. It was worse than I imagined.

The island was littered with crushed beer cans. From the looks of it, he wasn't too loyal to a particular brand. If it said beer, he would drink it. The countertops had crumbs and spilled food sticking to them, and I don't think he'd done a dish in over a month. Two overflowing trash bags were sitting by the back door, waiting to be taken out.

I put my hand over my mouth and nose and tried not to breathe in too much. I quietly opened and closed drawers—the whole time keeping an ear out for any disruption in Shifley's snores. With as much alcohol as he'd consumed, I didn't expect him to stir for hours.

When I didn't find anything incriminating in the kitchen, I tiptoed back into the living room and started up the stairs where Aunt Shirley was currently poking around.

I found her upstairs in Shifley's extra bedroom.

"Would you look at what this nutso has in his possession?" Aunt Shirley held up a pair of white, satiny granny panties. Panties so big if you put them on they'd go up past your belly button.

"Eww. My gosh, is he *stealing* those from patients at the Manor?" I don't think I'd ever been so disgusted by anything in my whole life.

"I knew Shifty was weird," Aunt Shirley said, "but this is a whole new bag of crazy. He's got a fetish for old-lady panties!"

She held up another pair exactly like the first, only they were red. "I bet Old Man Jenkins would love me in these."

I plugged my ears. "Stop talking now, please."

I looked around the room and let out a soft whistle. From the looks of things, I'd say Shifley was definitely the thief at the Manor. I gazed out over the assortment of wallets, jewelry, and clothing that obviously did not belong to him.

I thought about what he'd said downstairs about being innocent. If he lied about this, was he also lying about not murdering Manning?

"So do you think he killed Manning?" I asked. "Maybe Manning found out what Shifley was doing and threatened to expose him if he didn't cut him in."

"I honestly don't know. I'm assuming you didn't find anything in the kitchen?"

"No. We have him for the theft, and in just a few hours Garrett will be here with a search warrant. So Shifley is going down for that at least. But we have nothing to prove he killed Manning."

Aunt Shirley walked over to an oak dresser up against a wall and pulled open a drawer. "Looks like quilts and afghans in here." Aunt Shirley lifted up one of the quilts. "I think this is one that Lovey and Dotty made. They're gonna flip when we tell them he's stealing their stuff from other people." Aunt Shirley shook her head in disgust. "Stealing from old people. That's a new kind of low." She pulled open the top drawer of the dresser. "Hey, I was needing a new pair of dentures. These look pretty good!"

"Put those down!"

I was about to suggest we get out before Shifley woke up from his drunken stupor when I heard footsteps on the stairs.

"In the closet!" I shoved Aunt Shirley into the closet, stepped in after her, and closed the closet door except for a crack for me to see through. I tried to calm my breathing and beating heart.

"I told you they ain't here," Shifley slurred into his cell phone. "They left when I told them to get out."

Guess again, jerk!

"I'll have everything boxed up and ready for the pawn shop by tonight. Stop worrying." He hung up the phone and staggered farther into the room.

I was beginning to feel claustrophobic. I willed Shifley to get out so Aunt Shirley and I could plan our escape. After touching a couple of the items, he turned and staggered back out of the room. I prayed he was going to his room to nap so we could sneak down the stairs and out the front door.

Of course luck wasn't with me. A few seconds later I heard him crashing, falling, and cursing his way down the stairs. A few more seconds later the TV began blaring.

"How're we gonna get out of here?" I whispered.

"Why are you whispering?" Aunt Shirley said and pushed me out of the closet. "That TV's so loud the neighbors have to be able to hear it."

"How are we going to get out of here without getting caught?" I repeated.

Aunt Shirley shrugged. "Climb out the window that was directly above the porch. From there we can slide down on our stomachs and dangle over the edge...then let go."

"Did you just think of that?"

Aunt Shirley patted me on my head like I was two years old. "Honey, first lesson in being a private eye...always have a way out."

"One, I'm not a private investigator. And two, I thought the first lesson was always have plenty of food on a stakeout."

Aunt Shirley laughed at my feeble attempt at humor. "Do you suppose he was talking to Sheri Daniels or Carl Baker on the phone?"

I shook my head. "I honestly have no idea at this point. But I'd say it's a for sure thing that one of them is his partner."

"Let's go. I want to get back to the office and figure out our next move."

I held up my hand. "Our next move is letting Garrett make an arrest. I'm leaning more toward Shifley being both the murderer and thief. I don't want to tangle with him anymore."

Aunt Shirley put her finger up to her lips and motioned me to be quiet. She tiptoed out of the stolen stash room and across the tiny hallway toward Shifley's bedroom.

I wrinkled my nose when we entered. It smelled like mildew meets week-old funk. I made a gagging noise before I could stop myself. Two of his Manor uniforms were wadded up at the foot of his bed on the floor. I assumed he just bent down and put them back on the next day.

I think his bed sheets were supposed to be tan, but they looked more like light green from the filth. There were sporadic burn holes in the sheets—presumably from cigarettes. Classy.

"How in the heck does he sleep in this smell and filth?" I asked, bringing my coat sleeve up to cover my nose and mouth.

Aunt Shirley crept over to the lone window Shifley had in his bedroom. She eased it up and slipped out onto the roof. "Let's go."

I had just slid my feet out onto the roof when I noticed a package of chocolate covered espresso beans on Shifley's nightstand. There was something about it I couldn't put my finger on.

"Let's go!" Aunt Shirley hissed again. "Someone is bound to see us up here if we lollygag."

I filed the clue away for a later day. At least I thought it was a clue.

CHAPTER 23

"How's your ankle?" Mindy asked.

I took the ice pack off to examine the swelling. Aunt Shirley's idea of just gracefully sliding off the porch roof and onto the sidewalk didn't work out so well for me. I landed hard on my ankle, then my butt.

"It's fine." And it really was. I just wanted Aunt Shirley to feel guilty for once again getting me into a ridiculous situation.

"You need to start working out more," Aunt Shirley barked from her desk. "You have no muscle tone and you have hamster strength. A drop like that should be nothing. Instead you practically break your ankle, hip, and butt. You're a disgrace to the job!"

"You sound like Hank."

"I never thought I'd say this," Aunt Shirley said, "but Hank's right."

I glared at her, then put the ice pack back on my ankle and went back to feeling sorry for myself.

"I know what will make you feel better," Mindy announced. "Valentine's presents!"

She opened her side drawer and pulled out a package wrapped in glittery pink hearts and lifted up a matching gift bag from the floor next to her desk.

"You got us Valentine's Day presents?" I started to panic. I hadn't gotten her anything. We'd never exchanged gifts before.

Mindy must have seen the look on my face because she waved her hand. "It's nothing big."

Mindy handed the gift bag to Aunt Shirley and I got the wrapped package.

"I gave the same gift to Paige when she was in here yesterday," Mindy giggled. "I figured it might help get that baby here faster."

I felt my face turn red. I'm not a prude by any means, but now I was scared to open the gift.

"Well, I'm not afraid to open my gift," Aunt Shirley said. She reached inside the bag and lifted out the gift then started to laugh. "I love it!"

"It's called a boozy bouquet," Mindy explained.

Instead of flowers inside a vase, there were twelve pointy sticks with tiny one-serving bottles of booze glued to the end of each stick. Greenery and baby's breath were stuck in the vase to hide most of the sticks and give it a decorative vibe.

"You know," Aunt Shirley mused, "I once thought I found true love when I was in my forties. That is, until we went out that night and he asked me if I thought I really needed another drink. I dumped him immediately. I don't need that kind of negativity in my life!"

Even though I laughed at her attempt at humor, tears filled my eyes. I suddenly felt like a crappy niece. Sometimes I get so used to seeing Aunt Shirley as a burden that I forget she's a woman with emotions. I felt like a heel for not getting her something for Valentine's Day. Here she was getting all excited over a gift of tiny booze bottles glued to a stick.

"Stop getting so sappy," Aunt Shirley snapped. "At least I have my date with a boozy bouquet tonight while you heathens are out having kinky fifty shapes of grape sex. I heard that's the thing to do these days."

Mindy giggled while I laughed so hard my side hurt. I wiped my eyes and smiled at Aunt Shirley. "That's not what it's called. And you've totally ruined any thought of that…ever!"

"Am I paying you to party or to write?" Hank yelled from his doorway. "Did you get the goods on this Shifley character?"

"I'm on it!" I yelled. But Hank had already shut the door on my reply.

"Hank's taking me to Kansas City tonight," Mindy whispered excitedly. "Hopefully we'll be a little late to work tomorrow."

Aunt Shirley and I laughed. Poor Hank had no idea what he was in for.

Plop! Plop!

I checked my phone and saw it was a text from Garrett. "Saw paper. Congrats to you on two front-page spots. We are celebrating you tonight."

I nearly groaned aloud in anticipation. I looked down at my still-wrapped package. Did I have the guts to open it here?

"Open it tonight when you are with Garrett," Mindy said. "Trust me. You both will love it."

"Thanks. I want to call Virginia real quick to remind her about the paper. Then I see no reason why we can't go by Mom's house to see how she and Paige are coming on our Valentine's desserts."

My mom was the best baker in Granville. At least I thought so. I, however, didn't inherit her baking gene. Garrett hardly ever let me live down the *one* time I accidently mixed up Cream of Tartar and Tartar Sauce. Now he begs my mom for desserts.

I opened my cell and dialed Virginia's number. It rang four times before her answering machine picked up. I left a message reminding her to make sure she read her front-page article in the *Gazette* and promised I'd stop by in the morning to get her reaction—hers and Lovey's and Dotty's. Over mimosas I was sure. I also wished her well on her date with Bert.

I parked the Falcon in Mom's driveway. Aunt Shirley and I rushed inside to see what goodies we'd be taking home.

I loved the house I grew up in. Mom had done some major remodels over the years, and her old Victorian had some great modern conveniences inside when it came to her kitchen and bathroom. My favorite update had been the library. The place that gave me my start for a love affair with words.

The library was one of the largest rooms in the house. It had originally just been two small rooms next to each other. Mom said back in the day, one room was probably a parlor and the other may have been a bedroom. She decided to knock the wall down and make it a huge library. All four walls were filled with recessed bookshelves holding hundreds of books. Along with the gas fireplace, she'd also added a large dome-shaped skylight for just the right ambiance.

"Smells divine," I said as Aunt Shirley and I walked in the back door of the kitchen.

Paige and Mom were sitting at the kitchen table, a bottle of sparkling wine between them. Chocolate dipped strawberries, Whoopie pies, and a pan of Mom's famous Slutty Brownies were sitting on the cabinet.

I poured a glass of sparkling wine for Aunt Shirley and me, sat down at the table, and plucked a chocolate dipped strawberry from the plate.

"Mmmm. Wonderful as always, Momma."

Mom leaned over and kissed me on my cheek. "Thanks. Paige and I are sure that tonight's desserts will get me a grandbaby!"

I laughed at Paige's red face. "Yes. I couldn't help but notice the desserts this year. Slutty Brownies and Whoopie pies, Momma? Could you be any more obvious?"

It was no different than my subliminal ho-ho cake roll I tried to make Garrett, but I wasn't going to admit it.

Unfortunately, Paige did. "I once remember someone attempting to make a ho-ho dessert!"

Mom grinned and took a sip of her sparkling wine. "All I can say is it's about time I was bouncing a grandbaby on my knee. Your brother is the oldest...*and* he's a male. He has a duty."

I laughed at her ridiculously sexist statement and took another drink to mask my delight. Thank God it was Matt getting the brunt of the baby lecture. While I was happy with my relationship with Garrett, I wasn't yet ready to bounce babies on my knees just so my mom was happy.

"Congrats on your two front-page stories," Paige gushed. "You must be proud."

I smiled. "I am. And Hank said if I can solve this case with the Manning murder quickly, he'd give me the next front-page cover!"

"I'm so proud of you, Ryli," Mom said.

"My nephew is about to graduate from the police academy and join up with the Granville Police Department," Aunt Shirley told Paige. "You need to start learning how to do pillow talk with your man. Get us some dirt we can use. Ryli ain't no good at it."

"What's on your agenda tonight?" I asked Mom, trying to steer the conversation away from where it was going. No use getting Paige worked up.

"Martin is taking me out for a romantic dinner," Mom sighed. "I haven't been out with a man since your father passed."

It wasn't hard to do the mental math. I knew how old I was, and the fact Mom didn't date while I was growing up made it an even easier tally. "Wow. Think you're ready for this kind of commitment?"

Mom slapped me lightly on the arm. "Oh, stop." I could tell by her blush she was excited.

"What time is he picking you up?" Aunt Shirley asked.

Mom looked at the clock on the wall. "In a couple hours. I hate to cut this short, but I should start getting ready."

Paige, Aunt Shirley, and I packed up our goodies and said goodbye. As I carried my chocolates out to the Falcon, I couldn't help but think how much our lives had changed over the course of a year. Matt and Paige were married, trying to have a baby. Mom was dating Doc, and I was dating Garrett. What a difference a year made.

Miss Molly greeted me at the door, once again meowing with rage at the injustice of having to wait for me in order to eat. I bent down to pet her as I made my way to the kitchen.

Once I fed Miss Molly, I poured myself a glass of sparkling lime water and went in search of just the right outfit for tonight.

Aunt Shirley was stretched out on my bed, reading a magazine, and pouting.

I rolled my eyes. "Don't pout just because I have a date tonight and you don't. I'm sure Old Man Jenkins would love to do something with you. You're the one choosing to stay in tonight."

"There's a murderer on the loose. Aren't you afraid they'll come after me tonight?"

I laughed. "No. I'd be more afraid for them than you!"

Aunt Shirley scowled at me.

I sighed and sat on the edge of my bed. "Listen. No one is going to try to come at you tonight." I took a drink of my sparkling water. "I'm sure by now Shifley has been arrested for the thefts, and everything will be wrapped up nice and pretty."

"Fine. Bring me a glass of that wine we got the other day and I won't whine anymore."

I went back into the kitchen and poured her an extra-large glass. I wanted her happy, but drunk and passed out would work, too.

I spent the next couple hours trying to take my mind off of what was going on down at the police station. I was practically chomping at the bit. I tried to read, but after rereading the same paragraph for the fourth time, I threw the book aside.

I went into the kitchen to refill my glass of sparkling water and decided to get ready. Since I hadn't heard from Garrett that tonight was off due to his having to work, I figured he'd already wrapped things up.

After picking out my outfit—a knee-length black dress with cutout shoulders and black boots—I ran a bubble bath. I poured in extra bubbles to ensure I smelled like vanilla lavender when I got to Garrett's house. It was his favorite scent after all.

I also took extra care with my hair, adding bouncy curls all over. As I was zipping up my boots, Aunt Shirley came out of the bedroom, empty wine glass in hand.

"Go easy on that," I cautioned. "I won't be here to pour you in bed."

"I've been drinking since before you were born. I'm sure I can handle two glasses of wine."

I snorted. "I've seen you after two glasses." I opened the refrigerator and grabbed the bottle of white wine I bought from the winery and slipped on my coat. Next I grabbed the tray of chocolate covered strawberries, Slutty Brownies, and Whoopie pies. Now the night was set.

Aunt Shirley sighed. "I'll try to keep my mind off the fact there's a killer running around and your man hasn't had the decency to put her behind bars yet."

I rolled my eyes at her. "You're back to thinking Sheri Daniels is the killer, huh? Okay. Well, just lock the doors, and don't answer if Sheri comes calling. Simple as that!"

Aunt Shirley stuck her tongue out at me, flopped down on the couch, and turned on the TV. "Don't do anything I wouldn't do."

CHAPTER 24

"Dinner was good," Garrett said as we stood at the sink drying dishes. He'd made lemon-basil shrimp, baby potatoes, and baked asparagus. He had not said one word all night about whether or not he'd arrested Thomas Shifley. "But the desserts were definitely the best part."

I reached up and stroked his cheek. "Hopefully not the *best* part of the evening."

Garrett threw the tea towel on the counter, gave me a wolfish grin, and backed me up against the refrigerator. He leaned down and kissed my neck. "I can guarantee you," he whispered in my ear, "the best part of the evening is yet to come."

I shivered. "Good."

He wrapped one hand in my hair and slowly rubbed his lips against mine.

The blaring of my cell phone shattered the moment. "It's just Aunt Shirley," I muttered against his mouth. "Ignore it. She'll go away eventually."

I felt him turn from me.

"No, no, no." I tried desperately to cling to him. No way was Aunt Shirley winning this battle.

"Actually," Garrett said as he kissed me quickly on the nose, "that's my phone. And I better get it. I'm waiting to hear back from the DA about something."

I instantly went on alert. "Did you arrest Thomas Shifley this afternoon for the thefts at the Manor? Is this on another arrest? Does this have anything to do with the Manning murder?"

Garrett chuckled and shook his head. "The police department has no comment on the questions." He slipped from my grasp and picked up his phone off the counter. "This is Kimble."

I was trying to figure out the best way to listen in when my cell rang. I marched over, snatched it up, looked at the number, and was ready to give Aunt Shirley a piece of my mind.

I didn't even get a chance to say hello.

"I need you to come bail me out of jail," Aunt Shirley barked.

My eyes darted to Garrett. He was staring at me while still on the phone. He lifted one eyebrow then shook his head at whatever was being said to him.

"What have you done?" I hissed into the phone.

"Just come get me. But let me tell you, that Officer Ryan is some great eye candy. I didn't even put up a fight when he patted me down."

I groaned.

"Don't worry, he was a sissy about it really. Kept saying he was just doing his job, muttering about what the Chief was going to do to him. But now I'm done looking at him and ready to go home."

I looked again at Garrett. His face was getting darker the more he listened. "Keep her locked up. We'll be there shortly."

There goes my celebration night.

"You deaf?" Aunt Shirley bellowed in my ear. "I said come get me."

"I'm assuming Officer Ryan is talking with Garrett right now," I said sharply. "You aren't going anywhere anytime soon. So just sit tight, and I'll get you when I can."

"Darn that Kimble! When I get my hands—"

I hung up mid-rant.

Garrett hung up and just stared at me...not saying a word. I hate it when he did that. I knew it was a police tactic to try and get me to spill my guts. I wasn't going to fall for it. I was stronger than that.

He narrowed his eyes and slowly moved toward me like a hunter stalking its prey. I folded like a lawn chair. I'd never be good in serious interrogations. "So you know she's in jail?"

Garrett didn't say anything, just nodded his head and kept walking toward me.

"How mad are you?"

Garrett chuckled humorlessly. "You have no idea."

I bit my lip and took a step backward.

His pupils dilated.

I stopped breathing. I knew that look. All thoughts of springing Aunt Shirley from the pokey fled. Looked like it was still going to be my night.

He flipped me over his shoulder like I was a sack of potatoes and carried me into the living room. I laughed as I bounced with his every step. "You and your aunt are sometimes more trouble than you're worth, Sin." He swatted me playfully before returning me to my feet.

"Too much on your aging heart?" I teased. I knew our age difference still bothered him a little.

"I'll show you old, Sin."

"I was hoping you would."

Yep, it was still gonna be my night!

✱ ✱ ✱

"Where have you been?" Aunt Shirley demanded when Garrett and I walked into the holding area an hour later.

She took one look at Garrett then looked back at me. "You engaged in hanky panky while I was rotting away in jail!"

Officer Ryan coughed and looked up at the ceiling. I was so embarrassed I wished the ground would open up and swallow me.

"That's enough," Garrett said. "I'm more interested in what you did to get here."

I wrapped my fingers around the bars and leaned in as close as I could and squinted at her. "What's wrong with your forehead? Is that a bruise?"

"Police brutality." Aunt Shirley crossed her arms over her chest and glared at Officer Ryan.

"Sir, that did not come from me," Officer Ryan said. "She actually did it to herself."

"So *you* say," Aunt Shirley hollered. "For all I know you did it to me when you shoved me into the police car."

I rolled my eyes at her. "Wouldn't you know if he hit your head on the car door?"

Aunt Shirley averted my eyes. "I may not have been conscious when he put me in the car."

Garrett held up his hand. "Start at the beginning, Officer Ryan." Garrett turned and pointed at Aunt Shirley. "And I don't want to hear one word from you."

Aunt Shirley waited until his back was turned and stuck out her tongue. Officer Ryan's eyes bulged out of his head.

"Officer Ryan?" Garrett prompted.

Officer Ryan cleared his throat and looked back at Garrett. "It seems Ms. Sinclair's neighbor, Miss Mabel, came by to drop off Valentine's Day cookies to Ms. Sinclair tonight."

"My ninety-year-old neighbor?" I looked at Aunt Shirley when I said it.

"Yes, ma'am. Miss Mabel came bearing gifts and it seems your aunt mistook her for a burglar."

I clutched my heart. "Omigod. Tell me Miss Mabel is okay!"

"She's fine. It was just a little scare." Officer Ryan cleared his throat and shuffled his feet. "Anyway, Miss Mabel said she saw Ryli leave and figured she was going out so she'd just put the cookies on Ryli's table." He turned to me. "She said you gave her permission to use the key under the doormat whenever she wanted."

Garrett looked at me. "You keep an extra key under your mat? Are you purposely trying to get robbed?"

"I say the same thing," Aunt Shirley said disgustedly.

Seeing as how we just broke into someone's house doing the same thing, I thought Aunt Shirley had a lot of nerve.

Officer Ryan bit back a smile. "So anyway, when Miss Mabel was bent over retrieving the key, Ryli's aunt opened the door. Now, your aunt claims to have mistaken Miss Mabel for Sheri Daniels. Who, by the way, your aunt keeps insisting murdered Ray Manning, and we should be ashamed of ourselves for letting her roam free."

"The bump?" Garrett sighed wearily.

"Well, according to the statement I took from Miss Mabel, Ryli's aunt had nunchucks in her hand and was swinging them around wildly when Miss Mabel stood up. One of the sticks came back and hit Ryli's aunt in the forehead and down she fell. Again, all this is according to Miss Mabel."

"I *knew* you'd hurt yourself with those stupid things," I said.

Garrett turned to Aunt Shirley. "When did you get nunchucks?"

I figured I'd better answer to save Aunt Shirley from a lecture. "Aunt Shirley, Paige, and I went to Locked & Loaded yesterday to get your Valentine's Day gift. Which, by the way, is still in the Falcon's trunk."

I added the last part hoping he'd go easy on us all if he knew he still had a gift coming.

One side of his mouth lifted. "Nice try."

Darn.

"That's their version," Aunt Shirley said. "Don't suppose you wanna hear mine?"

Garrett let out a small laugh. "Hardly."

"I still maintain your officer could have given me the goose egg."

"How about I take her home now?" I volunteered.

"Did Miss Mabel want to press charges?" Garrett asked.

I sucked in my breath. Surely sweet Miss Mabel wouldn't do that.

Officer Ryan turned to me. "Miss Mabel told me that as long as you called her and let her know you were okay, she would be content with forgiving everything."

"I'll call her now." I took out my cell and pulled up Miss Mabel's number. Turning my back on the group, I walked over to the opposite side of the room. I quickly explained to her that I was okay and that my aunt was staying with me for a while. I thanked her for the cookies and promised to call on her within the next few days.

"Miss Mabel is satisfied," I said. "Can I take Aunt Shirley home?"

Garrett cursed and unlocked the cell. "Fine. Take her before *I* decide to press charges."

"Ha!" Aunt Shirley said. "I should be the one pressing—"

I grabbed her arm and hauled her out before she could finish. I knew that tone, and no way did I want to tangle with Garrett at this moment.

I gave him a quick kiss on the cheek when I passed him. "I'll give you your Valentine's Day present tomorrow."

Aunt Shirley snorted. "Seems you already gave him a present, which is why I've been sitting in jail for the last hour."

I could hear Garrett growling as I tugged Aunt Shirley behind me.

CHAPTER 25

I was surprised to see Aunt Shirley up and dressed early the next morning. I figured she'd be sore and moving slow—what with her playing Whack-A-Mole with her head the previous night.

"We should go by and see what Valentine's Day candy they have on sale at the grocery store," Aunt Shirley said as she opened the refrigerator and took out an Ensure supplemental drink.

I snorted. "Miss Mabel was kind enough to still leave the cookies even after you practically accosted her. Eat those."

Aunt Shirley grimaced. "This is why I need to go back to living alone. In my own home I can eat all the chocolate candy for breakfast I want."

"From your mouth to God's ears. Hopefully Garrett will be arresting Sheri Daniels or Thomas Shifley today for the murder of Ray Manning and you can move back into the Manor."

"Until then, we stop and get candy on sale." Aunt Shirley picked up her purse. "By the way, did you find out if Shifty even *was* arrested yesterday for the thefts?"

"No. Garrett neither confirmed nor denied."

Aunt Shirley shook her head in disgust. "You are a disgrace."

I bit my tongue and fed Miss Molly her breakfast.

Our first stop was actually to the *Gazette* to see if Mindy had heard anything new with the investigation. She informed us that Thomas Shifley had been arrested for the thefts at the Manor. The police were still trying to figure out if he worked alone or with someone else. No one had yet been charged with Manning's murder.

"Funny how you're dating the Chief and my wife has more info than you," Hank said.

I ignored his remark. "So still no arrest for Manning's murder?"

"Not at this time," Mindy said.

What is taking Garrett so long?

We went to the store to get those tiny boxes of chocolate hearts on sale. Once we stocked up with a couple dozen boxes, we drove to the Manor to see if Sheri Daniels was even at work and see what gossip Virginia, Lovey, and Dotty knew.

I freaked when we walked by Sheri's office door and she was inside. I tried to hurry so we could pass without her seeing us.

"Because of you two I've been fired!" Sheri bellowed.

I groaned. No such luck.

Aunt Shirley snickered. "I'm not the one doing shady things!"

Sheri leaned across her desk, her face flushed. "If it's the last thing I do, I'll make sure you never return here."

Aunt Shirley did a little jig. "Jokes on you. As soon as you're arrested for the murder of Manning, Lucy Stevenson said I could come back."

Sheri's face went from red to white. She staggered backward and fell in her chair. "I didn't kill Manning!"

I was about to ask her who she thought did murder Manning when Aunt Shirley grabbed me by the arm and hauled me toward the elevator.

"Do you think it's true?" I asked. "Do you think maybe she didn't kill Manning?"

"Please, do you *honestly* think ole Shifty is capable of planning a premeditated murder? Because I don't."

She had a point.

"I hope Virginia liked her piece in the paper yesterday," I said.

We exited the elevator and made our way to Virginia's apartment. I figured Lovey and Dotty would already be there, and since it was ten in the morning, they probably were still having mimosas to celebrate last night's date night.

I knocked on the door and waited. When no one came, I knocked again, this time a little louder.

"Maybe she and Old Bert got down in the sack last night and she's still sleeping," Aunt Shirley cackled.

I frowned at her and knocked again. "Virginia, are you home?"

A door opened, but it wasn't Virginia's. Lovey and Dotty stepped out into the hallway.

"We were just on our way over," Dotty said. "We wanted to let Virginia sleep in a little this morning. She was exhausted after her date last night. Plus her stomach was still acting up."

Lovey nodded. "We had a nightcap last night when she got home from her date, and she told us all about her romantic evening. But then we cut it short because she wasn't looking very good. Earlier she had complained of an upset stomach before she left on her date, but we figured it was nerves. So we wanted her to rest a little this morning."

"I can't wait to hear all about it," I said. "And to hear what she thought of the paper yesterday."

Dotty clapped her hands together. "That's right! Congratulations! We read it together yesterday and it brought tears to our eyes."

"Well, unless this fabulous date contained some horizontal action, I could care less," Aunt Shirley said.

Lovey chuckled. "Which reminds me. Old Man Jenkins was asking about you yesterday."

Aunt Shirley motioned for more info. "What did he say?"

"Well, we stopped by to see if he needed anything. With it being Valentine's Day, Dotty and I were swamped trying to keep up with the demand."

"Yeah, yeah." Aunt Shirley rudely waved her arms like she couldn't care less. "What about Old Man Jenkins?"

Lovey chuckled, not offended in the least. "Well, he asked how you were doing, and if you were coming back anytime soon. We told him as soon as Manning's killer was caught you could come back."

Aunt Shirley preened. "He wants me. He wants me bad."

I groaned and turned back toward Virginia's door. "She's obviously still sleeping. I guess we should come back later."

Dotty laughed. "Nonsense. Sleeping Beauty's slept long enough. We really need her help to finish a quilt today."

I knocked again, but still no answer.

Lovey dug into her polyester pants pocket and pulled out a keychain. "Got an extra house key right here." She moved in front of me and inserted the key. The door unlocked and swung open.

"Virginia," Lovey called out sweetly. "Get your lazy bones up and come help us quilt."

No answer.

I looked over at the bar and kitchen area. The glasses from the previous evening's nightcap were still in the sink. A bowl of chocolates sat on the counter next to the decanters of booze.

I'm not sure why, but I suddenly got a bad feeling in my stomach. I looked at Aunt Shirley. She read me loud and clear.

"I'll just go get her up," Dotty said and started to walk down the hall.

"Hold up," Aunt Shirley said. "I'll go get her."

Dotty cocked her head to the side. "Why? I've seen Virginia in every state of dress and undress. She can't..." Her face turned white and her voice trailed off. Her eyes cut to Lovey.

Lovey was busy wiping down the counter. She looked at Dotty when she trailed off. "What's wrong Dotty? You don't look well."

Dotty lower lip trembled and tears filled her eyes. "They think something's wrong with Virginia."

Lovey looked at me then Aunt Shirley. She dropped the glass she was holding. It crashed to the floor and shattered. Lovey took off for Virginia's bedroom.

The four of us were pretty much on top of each other when we flung Virginia's bedroom door open.

She was lying on the floor, her red flannel pajama dress billowing out around her. Her normally perfect hair was tousled and damp. Her skin had a slick sheen to it.

Lovey and Dotty screamed and ran to Virginia. Dotty lifted her up off the ground. I pulled out my phone and called for an ambulance. I had them on speed dial because Matt used to work for them when he was an EMT. I gave them the info they needed, hung up, and called Garrett.

"Little busy, Sin. What's up?"

I didn't hesitate. "Virginia. Dead. Oak Grove Manor."

Cursing. "Did you already call it in?"

I could feel the shock beginning to set in. My teeth started chattering and my head felt foggy. "Yes."

"I'll be right there," Garrett said.

I hung up the phone and turned to the girls. Lovey and Dotty were cradling Virginia's head in their hands. Aunt Shirley placed her head on Virginia's chest as I knelt down beside them. I picked up her cold arms and tried to find a pulse.

"It's no use," Aunt Shirley said. "She's gone."

Lovey and Dotty let out a wail that broke my heart. I couldn't even begin to imagine how they were feeling. I'd only met Virginia this week, and I wanted to join them in their sorrow.

Not wanting to hamper anyone's entrance into Virginia's home, I ran to the front door and made sure it was open. I stood out in the hall and listened for the ding of the elevator. I began pacing the hall, wondering what could be taking so long. I finally heard the ding. I pressed myself against the hallway walls as four EMTs came rushing by with a gurney.

"In there." I pointed to Virginia's open door and followed closely behind.

I could hear crying as I huddled near the entrance of the bedroom. I looked over at Aunt Shirley. She was as white as a ghost. I let out a sob and put my hand over my mouth. I felt my legs give out from under me.

"Hold on there." Garrett wrapped his arms around me and carried me into the living room. He set me down on the couch and knelt on the floor by my feet.

"Thanks," I whispered as he wiped tears from my cheeks.

Lovey and Dotty staggered into the living room while Aunt Shirley brought up the rear. They sat woodenly on the living room furniture and refused to make eye contact with me.

"Is she gone?" Garrett asked.

He was looking at Lovey and Dotty, but it was Aunt Shirley who nodded her head. "I'd say she's been gone for a few hours now."

I felt sick to my stomach. "I should have stopped by this morning instead of waiting. Maybe I could have been here in time!"

Garrett put his hands on my knee. "Don't think that. I'll be back in a few minutes. No one move."

We all nodded. The grief was too raw to argue.

"I just don't understand," Lovey said. "Do you think it was a stroke or what?"

"A stroke doesn't do that to a person," Aunt Shirley said. "I'd bet a thousand dollars she was poisoned."

"Poisoned!" Dotty gasped. "When? How?"

I thought back to Virginia's whereabouts yesterday. "Do you think she could have been poisoned during her meal last night?"

"Possible," Aunt Shirley admitted. "But why? This doesn't make sense."

"I'll kill her!" Lovey's petite fists were clenched in rage. "If Sheri Daniels had anything to do with this, I'll kill her myself! Save the courts from prosecuting her!"

Even though I felt the same way, I didn't want to throw fuel on the fire. "Let's not jump to conclusions. I'm sure Garrett has everything under control."

"Normally I'd argue that point," Aunt Shirley said. "But right now I think Ryli is right. We need to let the police do their job."

I handed Dotty and Lovey a Kleenex from the box, and Aunt Shirley got up and poured a shot of bourbon in two glasses. I was almost tempted to have her pour me one.

"Here. This should help." Aunt Shirley handed them the glasses, and we watched as they each took small sips.

"We are going to be wheeling the body out," Garrett said softly from the hallway. "Do you ladies want to stay here or go to your place?"

"We'll stay here," Lovey said. "See this through to the end."

No one said a word as Virginia's covered body was wheeled through the living room and out the front door. My grief was so palpable it hurt to breathe. If I was reacting this way, Lovey and Dotty had to be beside themselves.

"I'm going to need to ask you all some questions," Garrett said. "Ryli, why don't you and Aunt Shirley go with Officer Ryan and I'll take Lovey and Dotty."

Aunt Shirley and I followed Officer Ryan over to Aunt Shirley's apartment. We went over our story about Virginia's date the previous night, our suspicions of poison, and how we found her this morning.

Garrett walked in as we were finishing up. "I went ahead and let Lovey and Dotty go back to their apartment for a while. I let them know I'd be calling them down to the station later this evening for follow-up questions." He looked at me and sighed.

"I'm going to go arrest Sheri Daniels. I can't formally charge her, but I have enough evidence to at least hold her twenty-four hours for questioning on the deaths of Ray Manning and Virginia Webber."

I couldn't even perk up at the thought of a juicy story. Not when it meant it came with the death of a new friend.

CHAPTER 26

"Let's wait here for a little bit," Aunt Shirley said, "and see if we can get a picture of Sheri coming out in handcuffs."

I smiled at her enthusiasm, but it felt wrong. My heart was still hurting from the death of Virginia. She was such a lovely woman. I felt equally horrible for thinking that at one time I thought she had committed Manning's murder. I obviously wasn't cut out for solving crimes.

We walked down to the lobby by the front doors. I figured Aunt Shirley was also hoping she would catch a peek at Old Man Jenkins if he was playing checkers by the fireplace.

I took out my phone and pulled up my camera just in case. It wasn't long before we heard a loud commotion coming from Sheri's office. We both took off running toward the sound. Officer Ryan was blocking the door, but I could hear Sheri yelling inside.

"How *dare* you come in here and arrest me for something I didn't do! I didn't kill Ray Manning, and I didn't kill Virginia Webber! How many times do I have to tell you that you have the wrong person? I suggest you take your worthless hides out of here and go find the actual killer!"

My mouth dropped open and I looked at Aunt Shirley. I knew what was coming next. Garrett was going to unleash on Sheri the likes she'd never seen before.

Aunt Shirley rubbed her hands in glee. "This should be good."

I actually felt like smiling.

A few seconds later a red-faced Sheri came stumbling out of her office, hands behind her back, Garrett guiding her. I lifted my phone and started snapping pictures.

Sheri zeroed in on me and started screaming and shouting obscenities at Aunt Shirley and me. She was like one of her rabid Chihuahuas.

A small group of residents and orderlies started gathering where we were standing, tittering and whispering. I knew this was the most excitement most of them had seen in quite a while.

Lucy Stevenson was standing behind the information desk with a look of pure horror on her face. I kind of felt sorry for her. How in the world was she going to spin this into something positive? Not only was there a burglary ring at her place, but now there'd been two murders. I couldn't see people knocking down the doors to move into the Manor anytime soon.

"Nothing to see here, folks," Officer Ryan said as he parted the path for the others to follow. "Go back to what you were doing."

I snapped a few more shots as they walked past us.

"You!" Sheri yelled at me. "This is *your* fault! You obviously lied and told your boyfriend I did this!"

I smirked at her. "Nope. Didn't say a word. Guess your actions speak for themselves."

Garrett's lips twitched, but he looked at me sternly. "Move along."

I gave him a wink and grabbed Aunt Shirley's sleeve. "I think we have enough pictures. Let's go. I'm starting to get a really bad headache."

We followed at a safe distance behind the chaos, hopped into the Falcon, and drove to Burger Barn. I needed a cola to help ease the dull ache in my head. And the cheeseburger, fries, and chocolate sundae would hopefully help, too.

By the time we got back to the *Gazette*, we had enough comfort food to feed a small Army. I tend to stress eat when I'm anxious…or sad…or worried…and on and on I could go.

"I heard another murder occurred and an arrest has been made," Hank said by way of greeting. "I'm assuming you two did what I pay you to do and got the story?"

I sighed and put the food down on my desk. Times like these made it hard to separate my personal life from my professional one.

"Don't give us too hard a time," Aunt Shirley admonished. "Not only did we *get* the story, but we were *involved* with the story."

She went on to tell him and Mindy that it was Virginia's body we'd found and about Sheri's subsequent arrest as I passed out food. Passed out mostly to my desk, but I did share a little with the others.

Hank whistled when Aunt Shirley finished her story. "So Sheri Daniels killed Ray Manning because he knew about the burglary ring—which means she must have been the ring leader. But why kill this Virginia lady?"

Aunt Shirley looked at me then back at Hank. "I've been wondering the same thing. I'm not sure I'm convinced of anything right now. But it was fun seeing Sheri arrested. Couldn't have happened to a nicer lady."

Hank picked up the cheeseburger I'd passed out to him. "Thanks for lunch. Now hurry and eat. I want at least an outline of a story before the end of the day." He turned and walked back into his office.

Mindy got up and came over to my desk where I was sitting and shoveling food into my face. "Take your time, honey. The story isn't going anywhere." She leaned over and hugged me.

Once I finished my lunch and felt the caffeine from the cola ease my headache, I decided to get to work. Aunt Shirley and I jotted down notes, and a few hours later I put together a pretty good article.

"I think I'm going to call it a day," I said to Mindy once I'd e-mailed my story to Hank. "I'm really tired. I know I should call Lovey and Dotty, but right now I don't have the energy. I think Aunt Shirley and I are just going to call it an early day."

"Of course," Mindy said. "And don't worry about tomorrow. I can cover anything important here."

Aunt Shirley and I didn't speak on the way home. I knew why I wasn't talking—I was too dang tired. I was beginning to worry why Aunt Shirley wasn't talking. I didn't think it could be anything good.

We changed into sweats and t-shirts immediately. I then called Mom to let her know what had happened. Paige was with her, so I had Mom put me on speakerphone while I filled them in on the day's events. With a promise that we'd be careful, I hung up the phone and started to make Aunt Shirley and me some hot tea. Once it was done I opened one of the tiny bottles of bourbon from Aunt Shirley's boozy bouquet and poured some in the hot tea.

"Why kill Virginia?" Aunt Shirley finally asked as we sat on the couch silently drinking our doctored tea.

"I don't know. Does there have to be a reason? Maybe Sheri was jealous of her. Maybe she thought…" The truth was, I couldn't think of a single reason why Sheri would kill Virginia.

"I'm going to take a bath," I said when I finished my hot tea. "Maybe that will help me think."

I pulled my hair up on top of my head, poured lavender vanilla bubbles into the water, and wondered if Garrett had gotten Sheri to confess to anything yet. I closed my eyes and let my mind wonder.

"I'm coming in," Aunt Shirley yelled as she opened the door.

Instantly awake, I sunk down lower in the now-tepid water. "What are you doing? Get out!"

"Get dressed. I think I've figured it out. No questions right now. I need you to call Garrett and see what he's doing. Don't let him in on the fact I may have solved this case." Aunt Shirley slammed the door closed. "Hurry up!"

I sighed and grabbed a towel from the rack and proceeded to dry off. I wrapped the towel around me and went to go get my cell phone.

Garrett picked up on the second ring. "Hey, Sin. What's up?"

I wasn't exactly sure what to say. "Not much. Just got out of the tub." I heard him groan and I smiled. "What's going on down there?"

"Sheri Daniels and Thomas Shifley are sitting tight in holding cells. Lovey and Dotty are here. I have a couple more questions I want to ask them about Virginia."

"Okay. Call me later when you're about to go home."

"Will do."

I hung up the phone and relayed my conversation back to Aunt Shirley.

"Perfect," Aunt Shirley said. "Let's go."

"I need to put clothes on! I'm still in a bath towel."

"We don't have time. We need to roll."

"Believe me…we have time for me to dress."

Ten minutes later we were at the Manor and hurrying inside. Luckily there were only a handful of people lounging around in the lobby. I assumed most had already eaten dinner and were calling it an early night.

"I don't understand what we're doing here," I said as I pushed the number three button in the elevator. "Did you forget something in your apartment?"

"No." Aunt Shirley unzipped her camo parka and pulled out a box from one of the inside pockets.

"What is that?" I asked.

"It's a kit to help you break into people's houses," she said matter-of-factly.

"No. I don't know what you're thinking…but no. I'm not doing this with you." The elevator doors slid open and emptied us out into her hallway. I refused to budge.

Aunt Shirley grabbed me by the arm and forced me to move. For an old woman she had some muscle.

I crossed my arms over my coat. "I'm not doing anything to anyone on this floor. I like the people for the most part. Well, except that mean Mildred. Is it her house we're breaking into?"

"No."

I sighed. "Then whose?"

"I want to look at something in Virginia's house real quick. Then I have one more stop in mind. But we need to hurry!"

As Aunt Shirley was bent over Virginia's door, which was covered in yellow tape, I walked over to Ray Manning's door and leaned against it. I was glad to see at least his yellow tape was gone. I crossed my arms over my chest and wondered what was so dang important inside Virginia's apartment that I had to put back on my flannel sweats instead of real clothes.

I heard a click.

"We're in," Aunt Shirley said. "Let's go."

I sighed and propelled myself off the door. Might as well humor her or we'd be here all night.

"Don't touch anything," Aunt Shirley warned. She took off for the bar and stood in front of the decanters filled with booze.

I strolled into the living room, trying not to be too creeped out by the emptiness of the apartment. I vaguely wondered what would happen to all of Virginia's nice things, and if Garrett called her children to tell them about their mom's death or if Lovey and Dotty did it.

Aunt Shirley picked up an empty bag out of the trash. She examined it carefully then shut the lid to the trash and walked over to the bar. She opened the top to one of the tiny containers next to a bottle of bourbon. She put her pinky in and tasted the powder.

"I was afraid of this."

The sound in her voice had me running scared. "What's wrong, Aunt Shirley?"

Before Aunt Shirley could answer, I heard the click of a gun.

"What's wrong is she's too smart for her own good."

CHAPTER 27

I turned around and saw Lovey pointing a gun at Aunt Shirley and me. Before my mind could register what was going on, Dotty came in behind Lovey.

"We can't do anything here," Dotty said. "The police may come back later tonight or tomorrow."

"I don't understand," I whispered.

"Me either. At least not fully," Aunt Shirley said. "So you two killed Manning and Virginia?"

"Sure did. We gave Virginia enough poison she should have died hours before she did," Lovey said. "Just like her to mess this whole thing up. We sneaked over around five this morning and she was still hanging on."

I felt hollow...like I was watching this scene unfold outside my body. My brain refused to understand what was going on. I hadn't felt this kind of fear in a long time.

"But you guys have been friends for sixty years," I protested.

Dotty grunted. "I think the term you young people use today is frenemy. We've been frenemies for over sixty years. She was easy to dupe. Virginia was never very bright."

Dotty walked over and picked up the jar Aunt Shirley had just put her finger in. I was afraid to ask what was inside.

Lovey made a motion with her gun. "Let's go. We'll take this party over to our place. Dotty wants us over there first. Good thing we caught on to your plan when you called your boyfriend."

"I was wondering how you got here so fast," Aunt Shirley said.

Lovey yanked me by the arm and turned me toward the door. "We heard Chief Kimble talking on the phone how he was going to ask us questions. We figured it was a rouse to see how much time you had to snoop around. So Dotty here faked a dizzy spell saying the day had been too much and could we please finish up tomorrow. Your boyfriend isn't much of a detective."

Now that pissed me off.

"As much as it pains me to say this," Aunt Shirley said, "you couldn't be more wrong. And when he goes over to Ryli's tonight, he's going to know to come here when he checks in with Ryli's mom and she's not there. This is the only other place in town Ryli and I would go. So you better think of something quick."

I couldn't believe Aunt Shirley had given away that much information. I was banking on the fact that Garrett was going to come looking for us soon.

Lovey and Dotty's apartment looked more like Aunt Shirley's than Virginia's. It was empty and sterile. They obviously meant to split after they killed us.

Lovey tapped me lightly on the head with her gun while Dotty pushed Aunt Shirley down hard on a kitchen table chair. "You text your boyfriend and tell him your aunt was homesick so you two decided to stay at her place. Tell him you'll see him tomorrow."

"Make sure you tell him to feed Ace," Aunt Shirley said. "You know how he likes you to talk about his new puppy he bought recently. Remind him that Ace is still a puppy and not that smart. He'll poop inside if not taken out regularly." She turned to Dotty. "He thinks if Ryli's good with a dog she'll be good with a baby."

I stifled a nervous giggle. No way was Garrett actually dumb enough to believe anything Aunt Shirley just said. But I now understood why she wanted me to text the secret message.

"Hurry up," Lovey snapped. "And I'm going to watch you so you don't do anything suspicious."

I took out my phone and swiped it open. I pushed on the text image. "Aunt Shirley is homesick. Since Sheri is in jail we're staying at the Manor tonight. I'll see u tomorrow. Auntie said to feed Ace. Ace is still a young pup & not that smart."

Hopefully the last part about Ace not being smart would bring him running. Now to keep them talking until the Cavalry showed up.

I just hoped Aunt Shirley knew *she* wasn't the Cavalry.

"Now that we have all night," Aunt Shirley said, "how about you tell us why."

"We don't owe you an explanation," Dotty said. She walked into the kitchen and took a knife out of a drawer. I had no idea what kind of knife it was, but it looked long and sharp.

Please hurry, please hurry!

"The why for Manning is easy," Lovey said. "We've known for quite a while that Thomas Shifley and Carl Baker were behind the thefts. You two aren't the only Nancy Drews running around here. If they had left our stuff alone, we would have left them alone. They want to steal from others, not our problem. But word got back to us they were stealing our quilts and afghans."

"Wait," I said. "So Sheri isn't the ring leader? I wonder if Garrett knows it's Carl Baker and not Sheri?"

Lovey shrugged. "Don't know. Don't care. We knew Kaylee had placed an order for castor beans for the greenhouse because they do every year around now to start germinating. It was just a matter of waiting until the perfect time to steal the boxes from the pantry. We chose to kill Manning because he wouldn't buy from us. And let's be honest, killing him was a community service if you really think about it."

"We're all about opportunity and taking it," Dotty said to Aunt Shirley. "We've been doing it for years. When you had the fight with Manning in the hallway, we knew it was time to strike. Whether it was Shifley or Sheri that got arrested was of no concern to us. We knew eventually Shifley would roll on himself—if nothing more than to save himself from a murder wrap."

"How did you know?" I asked Aunt Shirley. "What did you see at Virginia's that put it together for you?"

"The chocolates in the bowl on the counter. I wanted to see what the packaging looked like."

And then it clicked! I remembered seeing the same homemade bag of chocolates that Aunt Shirley had just removed from Virginia's trash in Manning's apartment. He was carrying them that day in the hallway when he was getting sick.

I turned to Lovey. "The first day we met in Aunt Shirley's apartment and you were showing me all the things on the cart, I heard you go next door to Manning's apartment."

Lovey laughed manically. "His special order of chocolate covered espresso beans was in the box when we stole the castor beans. Dotty and I dipped the castor beans in chocolate and then mixed them in with his regular bag of espresso beans we stole. We then put them in one of our bags so he wouldn't suspect anything. After a couple days of him not having any chocolates, we knew he'd buy from us. He bought his own death."

The bag of chocolates I saw in Shifley's room was a different brand. That's what confused me that day I was climbing out of his window. I was used to seeing the chocolates in a different kind of bag.

I could not imagine the kind of mind you'd have to have to steal a poison and just wait for the right time to kill and place blame.

"Why Virginia?" I asked. "She was such a lovely woman."

Aunt Shirley snorted. "Something tells me it's not the first time they've tortured Virginia."

Dotty threw back her head and laughed. "Right again! We've been torturing her since we were in school, she just didn't know it."

Lovey placed four glasses of liquid on the table. I thought it was hard alcohol of some kind but I couldn't be sure. I'll be darned if I was gonna drink it, though.

"Don't worry," Lovey said. "We'll answer all your questions, but first you need to take a drink. I'm sure you're parched."

I shook my head. "I'm not drinking anything."

Dotty picked up the knife and held it against Aunt Shirley's throat. I watched in horror as a trickle of blood ran down Aunt Shirley's neck. "Yes, you will. Or I'll slice her throat right here, right now."

"Better do what she says, dear," Lovey said nonchalantly. "Dotty has been itching to slice up your aunt for some time now."

My hand shook as I picked up the glass and slowly took a small drink. Aunt Shirley did the same.

"Your glasses are laced with enough crushed Ambien," Lovey said, "and whatever other sedatives we swiped out of people's cabinets while making deliveries, to pretty much kill you within a few hours of sleeping. So we better make it fast."

Where was Garrett?

"I'm getting hot," Aunt Shirley said. "Can I at least unzip my coat?"

"Whatever," Dotty snapped, turning the knife over in her hand for our benefit.

I wasn't sure what Aunt Shirley was up to, but I suddenly hoped she had a plan because Garrett seemed to be taking his sweet ole time. Aunt Shirley unzipped her camo parka and let it hang open.

"Now, Virginia is a totally different story," Lovey said and once again motioned for us to drink.

The creepy thing was they were drinking with us. Just like we'd all done a few times this week. These women were true sociopaths.

"I wish we had some popcorn to go with this story," Dotty said as she swirled her drink in her glass.

Lovey chuckled. "Virginia always thought she was better than us. Her first husband, Barry? He didn't die of complications from pneumonia. He was sick that day, yes. But when Dotty and I stayed up with him through the night, we were actually injecting him with insulin. In those days insulin was not what it is today. No one was the wiser. Not even my dad, the great Doctor Howk. Not Virginia, Barry's parents, no one! It was invigorating and addictive."

Dotty nodded and took another drink. "We found it was the perfect way to torture Virginia. Let her have a little happiness…and then yank that happiness away!"

213

"Drink," Lovey demanded.

I finished off the last of the drink and wondered when it would start to take effect. Where was Garrett? Had he not read my text yet?

"I think one more drink and then we can move them to Shirley's place," Dotty said gruffly. "I just wanted to make sure I had my favorite knife in case they needed persuading."

Lovey brought over the jar from Virginia's filled with the powder. She put four more spoonfuls of powder in our two glasses then topped them off with some bourbon.

"Now," Lovey continued, "Virginia's second husband, Stanley, that was a fun one. We sort of did the same thing we're doing here. We knew Virginia was out of town that night, so we decided to surprise him with dinner. We slipped massive amounts of crushed pills in his dinner and glass of Scotch, then waited for the pills to take effect. He was too doped up to realize what we were doing when we put the gun to his head with his own hand and made him pull the trigger. Sprinkle a few empty booze bottles around, and no one doubted for a second he hadn't committed suicide."

I gasped and felt my heart fall to my stomach. "Why would you do something so cruel? Virginia always thought she caused him to commit suicide. That's just horrible."

Dotty grinned. "I know. It tortured her for years. We couldn't have planned that one any better."

Lovey made a clucking sound with her tongue. "I did kinda of feel sorry for the kids. They were so upset. But I guess that's what happens when your mom thinks she's so much better than everyone else."

I couldn't help the giggle that escaped from me. If they seriously thought Virginia was a witch and she deserved what she got...these women were going to be in for the surprise of a lifetime when they died!

"And her last husband, Bob?" Aunt Shirley asked. "How did you manage that one?"

"You finish your drink and I'll tell you," Lovey said.

I wasn't sure if my sluggishness was from the two glasses of bourbon, the pills, or both. But I knew my senses were getting dull. If Aunt Shirley was going to do something, it needed to be soon. I looked over at the knife resting between Dotty and me. I wasn't sure if I'd be fast enough to take it from her. And if I was, could I actually use it?

Dotty chuckled menacingly. "Don't even think it, Ryli. I'd have you gutted before you knew what hit you."

I swallowed hard and nodded.

"Now Bob's death was perfect," Lovey said shaking her head and smiling. "My dad, the Great Doctor Howk, never gave me the credit I deserved. If only he knew how much potential I had."

For being crazy? If he was so great, something tells me he was aware his daughter was loopy!

Lovey leaned forward. "I knew Bob took a daily water pill. So it just made sense to kill him using potassium chloride." She turned to me and I could see the excitement in her face. "See I paid attention all those years in my dad's office. I knew pairing a water pill and large amounts of potassium chloride would be lethal. So the night of the party I mixed Bob's toasting glass and slipped in enough potassium chloride to mimic a heart attack but be untraceable."

Dotty clapped her hands. "Lovey always was the brains of the operation."

It's like I'm in the Twilight Zone!

"Ray Manning didn't send Virginia those threatening letters, did he?" Aunt Shirley asked.

"Nope," Lovey said. "Us again. Oh, the torture they brought her. It was delightful."

Dotty finished her drink and motioned for us to stand. "Let's go. You two are looking like you could fall over any second. Time to move you to your final resting place so Lovey and I can make our escape."

"But…why…kill…Virginia…now?" I could hardly talk around my tongue. At least that's how it felt.

Dotty slammed the pointed end of the knife down into the table. Aunt Shirley and I both jumped. "Because she went and got Bert! We would have let her live longer, but she did it to herself! It wasn't fair! Once again she was going to be the Cinderella of the ball and get the guy. Well, we made sure that didn't happen, didn't we, Lovey?"

They high fived each other and I almost vomited on the table. The more they talked the more I wanted to be physically sick.

"Sure did, Dotty. Virginia had outlived her usefulness anyway. We pilfered through her expensive jewelry to take with us as she lay dying, and we've got enough money to keep us afloat for a while until we decide where we want to go."

"Maybe one of those singles cruises for the elderly," Dotty said excitedly. "Could we do something like that, Lovey? I bet there are plenty of eligible men there."

Lovey nodded her head in agreement and pushed me toward the door. I tripped over my feet and fell on my knees. I was aware it hurt, but luckily my body was too numb to feel it immediately. Lovey grabbed hold of my hair and yanked me back on my feet.

"You don haf to hurt her," Aunt Shirley slurred. "We'll go."

"Let's go then," Dotty said. She turned and led the way toward the front door with Aunt Shirley behind her, then me, then Lovey pulling up the rear.

Everything happened so fast, I was pretty sure I was hallucinating. I heard Garrett's voice yell, "Police, open the door!" before the front door flew open, pieces flying everywhere. His gun was drawn and pointed straight at Dotty. Dotty began yelling and brought her knife up to stab him. I tried to scream a warning, but nothing came out. A shot rang out in front of me.

I didn't have time to process what was happening because Aunt Shirley whirled and pushed me out of the way. I stumbled backward and fell through the archway that led to the kitchen. Aunt Shirley reached into her parka and whipped out her nunchucks at the same time Lovey raised her gun to shoot Aunt Shirley. Aunt Shirley flung her nunchucks at Lovey's head. Lovey went down with a thud. Unfortunately, so did Aunt Shirley. She gave me a crooked grin, slid down the wall, and passed out with her mouth open.

Fearing she'd been shot and I was too doped up to hear it, I scrambled on all fours to where Aunt Shirley fell. I ran my hands inside her parka but didn't see any blood. My heart felt like it was being squeezed. I couldn't lose my aunt. As much as she was a pain in the ass…she was the best thing that had happened to me in a long time. The thought of her dying was incomprehensible. The room began to swim, and I knew I was starting to lose consciousness.

I felt Garrett slip his arms around me as I continued to stare at Aunt Shirley. I tried to speak but nothing came out. The room started to spill again and my stomach pitched. Garrett pushed the hair out of my face as I threw up all over his chest.

"Sleeping pills," I finally managed to whisper. Then promptly passed out.

CHAPTER 28

If you've never had your stomach pumped, consider yourself lucky. It was one of the worst experiences of my life. And I was once force fed ketamine by my preacher's wife.

Garrett later told me that he didn't see my text at first because after Lovey and Dotty left, he questioned Shifley one more time. That's when Shifley admitted that Carl Baker was his accomplice in the thefts. They were on their way to arrest Baker when he finally checked his phone.

When he saw the reference to Ace being a young pup and not that smart, he knew Aunt Shirley and I were in trouble. He called Matt and told him to go by my house while he and Officer Ryan went to the Manor to find us. It was just pure luck that he was breaking down the door when we were walking toward it.

Dotty had died before she hit the hallway floor. Matt told me later when Lovey finally came to and saw Dotty dead on the floor, she raged for hours. I didn't feel the least bit sorry for her crazy butt. I personally think she should have suffered a lot more seeing as how she tortured Virginia her whole life.

Lovey gave a full confession to Garrett. She admitted to poisoning and killing Ray Manning and Virginia. On the night Manning died, after Aunt Shirley and I had left the Manor, Lovey and Dotty had in fact gone to see Manning like they said. Only they didn't just deliver soup like they first claimed. They had ground up another lethal dose of ricin and mixed it in the soup, thereby ensuring that he would die that night.

Manning was too sick to notice that while Lovey gave him the soup, Dotty swiped his keys. Later that night when they figured he was dead, they went back over to his house with the stolen merchandise from the pantry and planted the stolen goods in his bedroom.

With the murder confession of Manning, Virginia, and Virginia's three husbands…Lovey Howk was guaranteed to never see the light of day again.

Virginia's two kids came to Granville to bury their mom. Aunt Shirley and I spoke with them to tell them everything we knew about their dad and his death. Even though they were still in shock over their mother's murder—and the fact Lovey and Dotty were involved—they seemed relieved to know their dad didn't kill himself like they always thought.

Aunt Shirley was back at the Manor, which was just fine with her. I, however, was having a hard time dealing with almost losing her. I promised myself I would change my attitude of seeing her as a burden. I vowed to have more patience with her in the future.

Even though she would never admit it, I think Aunt Shirley missed Old Man Jenkins. The near wipeout of her floor—Mean Mildred and the McElroys being the only ones left—meant Aunt Shirley was getting new neighbors. I wasn't looking forward to that. It still creeped me out to walk in the same hallway where Dotty was shot and killed.

Sheri was indeed still fired from the Manor. Thomas Shifley and Carl Baker were arrested and later convicted of the thefts of personal items from residents' rooms, and Kaylee Jones was free from bullying and threats at work. Interestingly enough, Big Baldy—the intimidating man in the workroom that told me to leave it be when it came to Kaylee—was actually trying to protect her. Seems he was in love with Kaylee and was just waiting for the right moment to rescue her from her predicament. The last time I saw her at the Manor she told me they had been dating for a few weeks now, and she couldn't be happier.

I wrote a tell-all story for the paper about my captivity and the confession Dotty and Lovey gave while they tortured us. Hank was in his element fending off calls from Kansas City newspapers wanting to interview me. I was once again his golden girl.

It wasn't until mid-March that things calmed down and went back to normal. Spring was trying to emerge, and now more than ever I wanted the old to die away and looked forward to something new.

"I've been thinking," Aunt Shirley announced one night at Mom's house during family dinner. "My birthday is coming up in April, and I sure could use a little vacation."

I looked at Garrett and tried not to groan. I didn't like the sound of this. It sounded like I could get in big-time trouble.

"And while I won't tell you my age, I will tell you it's a pretty important birthday. So I've been thinking of throwing myself a birthday bash at one of them WhoDunIt Murder Mystery weekend places."

Mom frowned at Aunt Shirley. "Haven't you had enough murder and mayhem in your life lately?"

Aunt Shirley waved her hand and dismissed my mom's comment. "I was thinking of making it a girls' thing. Janine, you can go." Aunt Shirley turned to Paige. "And Paige, seeing as how Matt ain't knocked you up yet, I see no reason why you can't go."

Paige's mouth dropped open. I laid my hand on her wrist so she wouldn't stab Aunt Shirley with the fork in her hand. "Then with me and Ryli going, it should be a fun weekend. What do you guys say? Wanna go solve a murder mystery for my birthday?"

I shook my head. "No, not really."

I looked at Garrett for help. He hid his grin behind his glass of sweet tea. Great, now I had an urge to stab *him* with my fork.

"I found one over by Hermann. We could do some wine tasting and participate in a pretend murder all in the same weekend."

I perked up at the words 'Hermann' and 'wine tasting.' Maybe this wasn't such a bad idea after all. A lot of wine and a pretend murder. I mean, really, how much trouble could we get into?

ABOUT THE AUTHOR

Jenna writes in the genre of cozy/women's literature. Her humorous characters and stories revolve around over-the-top family members, creative murders, and there's always a positive element of the military in her stories. Jenna currently lives in Missouri with her fiancé, step-daughter, Nova Scotia duck tolling retriever dog, Brownie, and her tuxedo-cat, Whiskey. She is a former court reporter turned educator turned full-time writer. She has a Master's degree in Special Education, and an Education Specialist degree in Curriculum and Instruction. She also spent twelve years in full-time ministry.

When she's not writing, Jenna likes to attend beer and wine tastings, go antiquing, visit craft festivals, and spend time with her family and friends. You can friend request her on Facebook under Jenna St. James, and she has a blog http://jennastjames.blogspot.com/. You can also e-mail her at authorjennastjames@gmail.com.

Jenna writes both the Ryli Sinclair Mystery and the Sullivan Sisters Mystery. You can purchase these books at http://amazon.com/author/jennastjames. Thank you for taking the time to read Jenna St. James' books. If you enjoy her books, please leave a review on Amazon, Goodreads, or any other social media outlet.

Made in the USA
Columbia, SC
25 August 2018